The Drifter

Stu Campbell

ISBN: 978-0-9988499-2-8

6   5   4   3   2

Edited by Mira Perrizo
Cover and text design by D.K. Luraas
Cover painting by R. Loren Schmidt

Printed in the United States of America

CHAPTER 1

The dust was pretty thick going down the road to the ranch. I closed the window on the car to keep the dust out. I thought that the road had gotten a lot of use during the dry spell. Some rain would certainly make conditions better, but too much rain would make a lot of mud and a feller could get stuck. I'd want to be careful driving to town on rainy days, if I went. However, it was early July and the threat of rain was pretty small.

I'd been told that this ranch was looking for some help for the summer—cowboys to do some riding work. I was a cowboy, looking for work. It appeared to be perfect, except for the pay. The pay was kinda low. I didn't have much money and anything I could make would certainly be welcome.

I drove the car up to what appeared to be the main house and waited until the dust I'd created coming down the road settled before I got out. I noticed that there was a fair amount of dust on the car. I parked beside an old truck that had seen better days. I wondered if it ran.

I got out of the car and went to the house. I knocked on the door but nobody answered. I knocked again and heard someone mumbling inside, "Keep your shirt on! I'm comin'."

When the door opened, I was met by an older man, obviously overweight. "What do you want?" he asked.

"I was told in town that you were lookin' for some help," I said.

"Who told you that?"

"That's what they said at the employment agency," I replied. I reached for the referral paper I'd been given at the agency. "They said to give you this." I handed the paper to the man.

He took it and looked it over, then said, "They called and said you'd be out. Come in."

I followed the man as he staggered into the living room. My first impression was that the house was dirty and not well kept. There was a desk in the living room, which apparently served as an office. There was a half empty bottle of bourbon on the desk and a half empty glass beside it. The television was on showing some game show.

"Have a seat," said the man, pointing to an old couch, as he staggered behind the desk and sat down. I noticed as he staggered to the desk that he constantly steadied himself by bracing against the wall or a piece of furniture.

I wondered if the staggering was because he was overweight or because he'd been drinking.

He almost fell into the chair behind the desk and reached for the half empty glass. He took a long drink, set the glass on the table and re-filled it.

Then he said, "Tell me about yourself."

"There ain't much to tell," I said. "Since I got out of the army, I've been cowboyin' an' bucka-rooin'. I've been out on the wagon on an outfit west an' north of here. I didn't want to help out in the hay, so I rolled up an' started lookin' for another outfit to ride for. I was told you were lookin' for riders."

"I could use another rider. I got two men working for me now, but they're kinda old. Can you ride colts?"

"Sometimes I ride 'em, sometimes I don't," I replied.

"Sometimes you don't. How come?"

"Sometimes they help me off!" I said.

"What do you do then?"

"Well," I answered, "I generally get up an' get back on."

I'd meant for my reply to be kinda humorous, but the man didn't see the humor. He simply said, "Oh."

The man reached for the glass and took a long drink. When he set it down, it was half empty. He never offered me a drink. I thought he wasn't too sociable. I would have turned the drink down if he'd offered me one, I don't think it's a good idea to drink during a job interview.

I was beginning to have some doubts about going to work for this outfit. The man appeared to be drunk and it was only mid-afternoon.

Before I could excuse myself and leave to go look for a better outfit to work for, he said, "I can use some help. Don't pay much, but I do furnish room and board. We'll give you a try on a trial basis. You can put your bedroll in the bunkhouse. You got a saddle?"

"Yep," I answered.

"You can put it in the barn. We'll get started about seven in the morning."

I had a job although I was kinda dubious about it. He told me where the bunkhouse was and I drove the car over to it and put my bedroll on an empty bunk.

The bunkhouse was dirty and it looked like it hadn't been cleaned for quite a while. There was a kitchen in one corner and a table with the breakfast dishes still on it. I saw a big saddle blanket hanging in the corner above the refrigerator. I wasn't impressed and had more doubts about working here.

I went outside and headed to the barn. There were some empty saddle racks in the barn and miscellaneous stuff scattered around. The barn was also a mess. Unimpressed, I went to the corrals and looked them over. There were a few horses in one corral and they looked to be in fair shape. I thought they ought to be out on grass, rather than in a corral eating hay.

I left my saddle in the car, not knowing if I was going to stay and went back to the bunkhouse. I sat out on the porch and had a smoke.

Presently, I saw two riders approaching from the north. They were coming down the same road I'd come in on and their horses were stirring up a lot of dust. I watched them ride to the barn, unsaddle the horses and turn them loose in the corral.

I didn't get up to meet them. I waited on the porch for them to come to the bunkhouse. I noticed them slapping dust off as they walked toward me. I could see that they were older men, pretty well past their prime.

They came to the bunkhouse and almost got there before they noticed me. When they finally did notice me, one of them asked, "Are you the new cook?"

"Nope," I answered. "I was told you guys could use some help. I'm just another buckaroo."

"Oh," said one of the men, sounding very disappointed. "We really need a cook."

"I ain't him," I said. "What are you doin' for a cook?"

"We don't have one so we been switchin' off on the cookin'. I'm George Cooper," said one man, stepping up and extending his hand.

I shook his hand and said, "I'm Pete Peterson."

The other man stuck out his hand and said, "I'm Davy Jones."

I shook his hand, repeated my name and said, "Davy Jones. That's a seafaring name, ain't it?"

"Yep," replied Davy. "But it fits out here. We're in the middle of a sea of dust!"

I said, "I came down the same road you came in on, but didn't see you."

"We saw your dust. That road provides a good signal when somebody's comin' in."

The men entered the bunkhouse.

"Come on in," said George.

"I did the dishes last night, so it's your turn to do 'em today," said Davy.

"No," said George. "I did 'em last night, so it's your turn today! You did the cookin' last night, remember?"

I could see what I thought was an argument developing and couldn't tell if it was serious or a good-natured argument.

"Your cookin' almost made me sick," continued George. "I'll do the cookin' today so I don't get sick."

"I suppose you're goin' to reheat that awful stew you fixed the other day," said Davy. He started to run water in the sink and wiped the dirty dishes off under the running water. He grabbed an old dirty towel and started to dry the dishes with it.

"What's wrong with it?"

"The meat ain't cooked an' the taters are almost raw," replied Davy.

"You know, too much cookin' takes the nutrients out of the food," said George.

I was becoming bored with the conversation, but didn't volunteer to help out. I was beginning to think I'd made a mistake hiring on with this outfit. It was too late in the day to move on. It was a long way to town and a motel room and a meal in town would cost too much money.

George reheated the stew. I was invited to eat with them. After their conversation, I wasn't sure I wanted to eat. But I was hungry and thought death from food poisoning would be better than starving to death. The stew was kinda bland and I only ate enough to avert starvation.

I went to bed early that night, not wanting to get into too much conversation with George and Davy. I could hear them arguing late into the night.

The next morning I was up early, before George and Davy. I was rattling things around in the kitchen, fixing my own breakfast. I only had the light on over the kitchen sink, washing the dishes I planned on using. Watching Davy clean and dry the dishes the night before convinced me that I needed to clean the dishes I ate off of.

The noise I was making woke up George. "What's goin' on?" he asked.

"I'm just fixin' some breakfast," I answered as I started the coffee.

"What time is it?"

"It's about five-thirty." I answered.

"We don't get started around here till eight o'clock," said George. "Go back to bed."

"I'm up," I said. "You go back to sleep. I'll fix my breakfast an' wait out on the porch for you."

I fixed up some taters, bacon and eggs and cleaned some dishes while breakfast was cooking. I felt fairly comfortable eating off what I knew were clean dishes.

As I ate, I surveyed my surroundings. The kitchen certainly wasn't clean. The sun was coming up over the mountains and what I had thought was a saddle blanket above the refrigerator the night before, upon closer inspection, turned out to be a giant spider web. It was covered with dust. I'd never seen a spider web that big before.

I'd about made up my mind to leave before I even started. However, I'd stayed at the ranch and ate their groceries and figured I owed them at least a little work. After I ate, I cleaned my dishes and stacked them in a corner, poured another cup of coffee and went out on the porch.

The lights weren't on in the main house and I figured I was the only early riser on this outfit.

I heard some noise in the bunkhouse and went inside to see who was up. I saw Davy starting his breakfast and he was reaching for the dishes I'd cleaned.

"Hold on there!" I commanded. "Those are

the dishes I cleaned an' I figured I'd use 'em tonight. They're clean! I ain't figurin' on doin' dishes for everybody!"

Davy looked a little embarrassed. "I'm sorry," he stated.

I don't think I endeared myself to him, but I thought I'd better get things straight in the beginning. I got another cup of coffee and watched, silently, as Davy put my dishes back.

Soon, George got up and Davy told him, "Leave them dishes in the corner. They're Pete's an' he's kinda fussy about 'em."

"Not fussy," I said, "just sanitary."

I watched as the men fixed their breakfast without saying anything.

After breakfast, we went to the corrals to catch the horses.

"You ride that sorrel, Pete," said George. "He's a little tough an' might buck some when you get on him."

I got my saddle, blankets, and bridle out of the car and lugged them to the corral. I caught the sorrel, hobbled him and saddled him. He humped up some when I tightened the cinch.

I untracked him, cheeked him and stepped on. He took one jump when I hit the saddle, but didn't do anything else. I rode him around in the corral to take the kinks out of him and to see how he handled. He didn't handle all that good—he didn't turn good and needed some work on his stopping.

While I was checking the horse out, George said, "I guess the boss is up by now. I'll go up an' see what he's got lined out for us to do."

I asked, "Don't the boss come to the corrals to give orders for the day?"

"No," replied Davy. "He's either in the house, doin' what he calls office work or out in the pickup watchin' what we're doin'. He's too fat to ride."

I thought, *That's a different way to run an outfit.*

George returned and said, "He wants us to gather all the cattle that are south an' move them to the west range."

"Is he drinkin' again?" asked Davy.

"Yep," replied George.

"It's a little early to start that, ain't it?" I asked.

"Yeah, but the time of day don't make no difference to him," answered George. "If he's up to it, he'll drive up on that far ridge in the truck an' watch what we're doin' with field glasses. He'll have his bottle with him."

"Pretty heavy drinker, is he?" I asked.

"Yeah," replied George. "I think that's about

all he eats, if you can call that eatin'. He'll go to town about every three weeks an' buy more booze. He buys it by the case."

I was definitely having some real serious doubts about staying on with this outfit.

"How come you guys stay on workin' for a drunk?" I questioned, as we rode our horses out.

"The work's pretty easy," said George. "Generally the boss leaves us alone, except for the spyin' from a ridge. We've got some gentle horses to ride an' we're both too old to go out an' look for another job. He pays regular, if we remind him."

"I can't leave," said Davy, "I ain't got no transportation. The only time I get to go to town is when I volunteer to drive the boss because he's too drunk to drive himself."

We headed out to the south, starting out at a walk. We got a few miles from the barn and George sent me out.

He said, "Gather all the cattle you can find an' push 'em to the west. Davy an' me will go farther south an' push what we find to the north an' west. There's a gate a few miles west of here. If you get there before Davy an' me, wait for us, but we should meet up with you before you get to the gate."

"Fine," I said.

I headed out toward the west. I didn't much care for the horse I rode. He was a head tossing son of a gun. I figured he'd been ridden with a pretty tight rein and was trying to relieve the pressure from the bit in his mouth. I gave him a looser rein and he slowed down on the head tossing, but he still tossed his head every time I tried to turn him by neck reining. He didn't respond to any leg cues. He didn't respond to much of anything.

I thought this horse needed a lot of riding and constant training and reinforcement at the same time. With a lot of training, he might be a pretty fair horse.

I found cattle and pushed them west. After a time, I saw a lot of dust being raised along a ridge. Remembering what had been said about the boss coming out in a truck to see how things were progressing, I figured it was him coming out to check his riders.

Soon, I met up with Davy and George. They mixed the cattle they'd gathered with what I'd gathered.

"You found a lot of cattle," said George. "More than what Davy an' I got. I figured you'd get plenty."

"I just brought what I came across," I said.

"I'll slip ahead an' open the gate an' get a count on 'em," said George. "The boss will want to know."

"I think I saw his dust up on the ridge," I said.

"Yeah, I saw it too! He's doin' what he thinks is his job."

When George left to open the gate, Davy and I backed off the cattle a little. We didn't want to crowd them and make George's count difficult. I slipped up toward the head of the herd so I could slow them down if necessary.

As George was counting the cattle, I started listing the reasons I didn't want to stay on with this outfit.

First, I thought, *there's the cookin'. It ain't really too sanitary. Second is the kitchen. It ain't too sanitary either. That big spider web in the corner is a sure sign of that. Third, there's the horses. I'm not really impressed with what I was riding today. I haven't hired on to train horses, there ain't enough money for that. Fourth, is the boss. He's a drunk an' I don't really like the idea of him comin' out an' spyin' on us every day. Fifth, there was a lot of meaningless talk between George an' Davy.* I concluded that I'd be better off leaving and the sooner the better.

Davy and I pushed the remaining cattle through the gate. George got his count and we started a leisurely ride back to the barn. It was supposed to be leisurely, but my horse was real chargy and I had to keep slowing him down. It was not a leisurely ride for me.

At one point Davy said, "Pete seems to be gettin' along good with that horse."

"Yeah," replied George. "He ain't givin' Pete the problems he's given the others."

I didn't say anything. I'd been riding the horse with a loose rein and he wasn't tossing his head as much. But I was having to check the horse more than I liked.

As we rode, I kept an eye on the dust coming off the ridge. All of the sudden, the dust stopped.

"There's somethin' goin' on up there," I said, pointing to the ridge.

Davy asked, "What?"

"I dunno," I answered. "The dust just stopped. We better ride over an' see what's happened. The boss might need some help."

We rode toward where I'd last seen the dust. Presently, we saw the truck, upside down in a small wash.

George spurred his horse into a run toward the truck. Davy was quick to follow. My horse didn't want to be left and followed Davy's horse as fast as he could go.

George made a flying dismount as his horse slid to a stop and ran to the overturned truck. He didn't stop to hobble his horse and the horse was loose.

"Don't anybody smoke!" hollered George. "There's gas leaking out all over here! The boss is still in the truck!"

Davy tried to catch George's horse, but without success.

"Leave him be!" hollered George. "Help me get the boss out before this thing blows up!"

Davy got off his horse and hobbled him.

"Hurry up!" prompted George.

My horse didn't have good brakes and I had a hard time stopping him—I was having a runaway. I had to circle him around a couple of times and finally decided to head him toward the truck. He'd either have to stop or crash into the truck.

The horse didn't crash into the truck. He stopped before he hit it. As fast as we were going as we approached the truck, I thought he was going to jump it, but he didn't.

George and Davy were trying to pry the driver's side door open without much success. I went to the passenger side and got that door open. In their rush to get to the boss, they hadn't looked at all their options,

"Here fellers, this door's open," I said.

George rushed around the truck, pushed me aside and climbed into the truck. The boss was sprawled out in the cab. I couldn't tell if he was alive or dead.

"Is he dead?" I asked.

"Nope," replied George. "He's just passed out. Give me a hand gettin' him out."

George and I dragged the boss out, feet first. He was heavy and we struggled to get him out.

When the boss was finally out of the truck, George said, "Better take him farther away. That truck's liable to blow!"

I started to drag the boss by the feet and George said, "Take him by the arms!"

We both dragged the boss away from the truck. When we had him to what we considered a safe distance, I asked, "Is he hurt bad?"

The boss had some scratches on his face. It looked pretty serious.

"I dunno," said George. "I doubt it. It's pretty hard to hurt these drunks. There's a lot of blood on his face. I'll clean him up as best as I can. There's not much I can do for him here. Davy, where's my horse?"

"He's headed out," answered Davy. "Probably at the barn by now."

George let out a string of cuss words, then said, "You better ride back to the ranch an' bring out the other truck. We need to get him home then figure out what to do. Don't bother to un-saddle your horse, just get the truck an' hurry back here!"

Davy left and George looked through the truck for a canteen with some water so he could clean up the boss. He found what he was looking for and went to cleaning up the boss.

I looked around for my horse. He was graz-ing where I'd hobbled him. I started toward him and George stopped me.

He asked, "Where you goin'?"

"Just goin' to check my horse," I replied.

"You better wait here," said George. "We'll need all the help we can get, loadin' the boss in the truck."

Davy got back with the other truck about two hours later.

"Where we goin' to put him?" asked Davy.

"I think it'll be easier to load him in the bed of the truck," replied George. "Come on, let's get started."

It took all three of us to get him loaded in the back of the truck and about half an hour to do it. With all three of us lifting, pushing, shoving, and pulling, we finally got him loaded.

When the job was done and George was closing the tailgate, I said, "I should have gone with Davy an' brought the front end loader back! It would have been a lot easier!"

George said, "Get your horse, Pete. We'll wait till you catch him an' get mounted before we leave."

I caught the horse and got on without any trouble. George saw that I was horseback, so he started the truck and left. The way George was driving, I determined he wasn't too concerned about the welfare of his passenger in the back. Davy waved from the passenger side of the truck as they left.

On the way back to the ranch, I made my plans. I'd unsaddle my horse by my car, put my saddle and equipment in the car, roll up my bedroll and leave. I was totally unimpressed with this outfit.

I rode into the ranch about an hour and a half later.

Davy saw me and called from the porch of the bunkhouse, "Supper's ready!"

I ignored him and turned my horse loose. I

put my bridle in the car and went to the bunk-house.

Davy was eating at the table. He was alone.

"Where's George?" I asked.

"He took the boss to town. Your supper's on the stove."

"I ain't eatin'," I replied. "I'm goin' to roll up an' leave."

"Why?" asked Davy. "You got along with that horse better than anybody else."

"It ain't really the horse," I said.

"Then why?" questioned Davy.

"I don't like playin' nursemaid to the boss," I answered. I didn't want to tell him I didn't like his cooking or the condition of the kitchen.

"The boss ain't here to write you a check," said Davy.

"That's all right," I replied. "I ate your gro-ceries an' slept in your bunkhouse. I figure a day's work is worth that." I wanted to add, "An' I figure I'm over payin' you," but didn't.

"Where you goin'?" asked Davy.

"Dunno."

"I kinda wish I was goin' with you," said Davy.

"I travel alone," I replied.

I rolled up my bedroll and headed to the door. "Hope your boss is okay," I said as I walked out.

"He'll probably be okay if he survives George's drivin'," answered Davy. "Good luck!"

I didn't answer, wanting to get away as fast as possible.

I got to the car, put my bedroll in the trunk and drove off. Davy waved as I drove off.

CHAPTER 2

There I was again, out of a job and looking for another one. But the first thing I was looking for was a good meal. I got into town and stopped to eat at a steakhouse. I'd seen the signs for this steakhouse along the road and pulled in. The place was crowded.

I was waiting for a seat when I saw George waving me over to his table. I went over and joined him.

"How's the boss?" I asked.

"They say he might survive," said George. "He didn't have any serious injuries from the roll-over. The doctors were more concerned about the alcohol level in his blood. They pumped his stomach an' gave him some plasma or somethin'. They said if he didn't quit drinkin' he'd die."

"I'd have thought the ride you gave him from the rollover would have killed him," I said, smiling.

George didn't laugh. "I've seen him in that condition before an' it ain't funny. This ain't the first time I've brought him to town passed out. You come to town to see how he was doin?"

"Nope," I said. "I'm leavin'."

"Oh?"

"Yep."

The waitress came and I ordered a big steak, medium rare.

"Can't say as I blame you," said George. "You ain't the only one that's left because the boss is a drunk."

"That's the biggest part of it," I said.

"I'll pay you a day's wage," said George. "The boss ain't in no condition to write a check."

"Forget it," I said. "I ate an' slept in your bunkhouse. I figure we're even."

George reached in his pocket and brought out a roll of cash. "I'll pay you. The boss will pay me back."

"That ain't necessary," I said.

"Well," said George, "I'll pick up your supper tab."

"Okay, you can do that if you want, thanks. How come you stay on with that outfit?"

George replied, "The boss is a distant relative. I told the family I'd look out after things

23

out here. I didn't figure on lookin' out for the boss."

My meal came and I started eating. George had finished his supper and got up to leave. He stuck out his hand and I started to get up to shake it, but he pushed me back down in my chair.

"Keep eatin'," he said. "Good luck!"

He took my bill and I saw him at the cash register, pointing over at me.

I finished my supper and went to the cash register to make sure everything was all right.

"That other cowboy paid your bill," I was told.

I left the steakhouse and found a motel where I could spend the night and get a shower. As I entered the motel room, I noticed that the there weren't any spider webs in any of the corners. I laughed at my relief.

The next day, I set out to find another job but I didn't find much. There were a couple of truck driving jobs available. I wasn't interested. There were some waiter jobs open, but I didn't think I could carry a big tray of food with one hand over my head. I could have gotten a job washing dishes, and while I did a good job of cleaning my dishes at the last outfit I worked on, I wasn't interested. I moved on to the next town to look.

CHAPTER 3

Two towns later, I was talking with an old cowboy over a cup of coffee in a café. He told me of a job breaking colts at a horse ranch some thirty miles out of town. I got directions to the ranch and after some driving around, I found the place.

I looked up the ranch foreman, introduced myself and asked him, "I heard you were lookin' for someone to break colts. Is this true?"

The foreman told me his name, Charlie, as he sized me up. I sized him up. He was about six feet two, and sunburned. He took off his hat and scratched his head. He had a definite farmer's tan. His forehead was pure white above where his hat kept the sun off. I almost laughed at his sunburn contrasting with his pure white forehead.

His hands were big and he had a strong grip. I figured he weighed about two hundred pounds.

"We do have some colts to break," he said. "I'll take you over to where they are an' you can look 'em over."

I followed Charlie to a corral behind the barn and saw a bunch of yearling colts in the corral.

"These are what we have. They need to be halter broke and gentled."

I looked the colts over. They moved to the far side of the corral as we approached.

"There's a dozen. They're all wild, never been handled," said Charlie.

I could tell they were mustangs from the freeze brands on their necks.

"Mustangs, huh." I made the statement rather than a question. "Did you catch 'em off the desert?"

Charlie laughed. "No," he said. "We have a deal with the BLM to gentle 'em down an' halter break 'em. The feller that generally halter breaks my colts broke his leg an' can't work. He's hobblin' around here on crutches. I need them halter broke by the first of September."

"I thought the BLM was dealin' with the prison system for that," I said. "Is this a prison honor farm?"

Charlie laughed again. "No," he replied. "The BLM manager, he's a good friend of mine, he thought if these colts were halter broke, they'd bring a better price at the BLM auction in September. Have you worked a lot of colts?"

"I've never worked on a horse ranch, but I've broke a few horses. It just takes time an' a lot of ridin'."

"These colts are too young to ride," said Charlie.

"I can see that," I replied. "All they need is a lot of ground work. What are you payin'?"

Charlie told me what the wage was. It was kinda low, but he added, "We'll furnish room an' board. If you want the job, you can put your bedroll in the bunkhouse."

As I looked over the colts, I considered my options. I was out of a job, looking for one and one was being offered to me. It wasn't a riding job, but it was a job involving working with horses.

"What's the cooking like?"

"The farm hands ain't been complainin'," said Charlie. "If you take the job, you'll bunk with the farm hands. That's where Bob stays."

"Bob?" I asked.

"Yeah," replied Charlie. "He's the hand that broke his leg."

"You got enough halters to fit all these colts?" I asked.

"Yep," answered Charlie. "An' lead ropes to boot!"

"The handlin' might be kinda rough to start with," I said.

"I understand," said Charlie. "But these are mustangs an' they can take it."

"I'll take the job an' start in the mornin'," I said.

"Good enough! Remember, I need them all halter broke by the first of September. That gives you a little over a month. If you do a good job, there'll be a bonus for you then. I'll show you where the bunkhouse is. Get your bedroll. You can park your car behind the bunkhouse."

I got my bedroll out of the car and followed Charlie to the bunkhouse. I picked an unused bunk in the corner.

Bob was in the bunkhouse, his broken leg propped up on a chair, watching television. His leg was in a cast. He was an older cowboy and I figured his riding days were about over. I thought he was a pensioner on this outfit.

Introductions were made and Bob appeared to be a cordial sort of person.

"Bob can show you where the kitchen is an' kinda acquaint you with the procedures here.

I've got work to do in the office," Charlie said as he left.

"What you figurin' on doin' here?" asked Bob.

"I'm goin' to halter break a bunch of colts," I replied.

"The rangs," said Bob. "That's my job here, I guess Charlie can't wait till I get out of this cast to do it."

"He said he needed 'em broke by the first of September," I said. "When you goin' to get out of that cast?"

"Not till sometime in October, accordin' to the doctor," replied Bob. "But I can come out an' help you some."

"I don't think Worker's Comp wants you doin' anything," I said. I was thinking, *I sure don't want a cripple in that corral with a bunch of mustangs that ain't been handled!*

I asked, "How'd you bust your leg?"

"My horse fell an' I couldn't clear the stirrup. I was holdin' the horse down 'cause I didn't know if I was still caught up in the stirrup. It took Charlie an' the other boys a while to get me free."

"I'll bet it hurt," I stated.

"Sure enough it did," replied Bob. "The ride into town wasn't no pleasure ride either!"

I immediately thought of the boss on the last outfit and George driving him to town. I didn't think the ride in the back of the pickup was very pleasant for him.

"I don't know what you can do to help," I said. "Those crutches are liable to get in the way."

"I can work around 'em," replied Bob.

"I heard this was a horse ranch," I said, wanting to get Bob off the subject of helping me. "But I ain't seen no horses. Where are they?"

"They got two stud bunches here," answered Bob. "One bunch is on the west side of the ranch an' the other one is on the east side. One is made up of registered Quarter horses an' the other one is registered Paint horses."

"There ain't no cows here?" I questioned.

"They got cows out south," replied Bob. "We were headed out to check on 'em when I broke my leg. Because of my wreck, we didn't get 'em checked that day."

"Where's the other hands?" I asked.

"They're all out irrigatin'," said Bob. "They'll be in around supper time. You got to be a jack of all trades to work here year round."

When I heard that, I was glad I'd only hired on to halter break the mustangs. I didn't much care for irrigating, hauling hay, or other ranch work.

"How's the cookin'?" I asked.

"Not bad. I've been on some outfits where it's better an' some outfits where it's worse. The cook is kinda ornery. It's best to stay on the good side of him."

Bob wasn't telling me anything I didn't already know. It's best to stay on the good side of any cook, regardless of how good or bad he is.

I parked my car behind the bunkhouse with a few other cars—I figured they were the hired help's—then went back into the bunkhouse.

Bob and I chatted until the other hands came in and the cook called us to supper. Bob introduced me to the other hands and we sat down to eat.

Supper was what the cook called goulash. It was hamburger, noodles, tomatoes and whatever else the cook needed to clean out his refrigerator. I didn't think it was too bad, but I could see some obvious dislike on the faces of the other hands.

After supper, I was ready to go to bed, but Bob wanted to talk. He questioned me about my past, where I'd been and where I'd worked before. It turned out that he'd worked on some of the same outfits I'd worked on before and knew some of the men I'd worked with. The more he found out what we had in common, the more he wanted to talk.

I finally put an end to the conversation by saying, "It's time I hit the sack. I've got to work tomorrow."

Bob looked at his watch, looked out the window and said, "You're right, it's well past dark!"

The other hands had gone to bed and were asleep. I suppose they just ignored Bob's conversations.

As I climbed into bed, I thought, *He's a talker.*

The next morning after breakfast, Bob followed me out to my car on his crutches. I opened the trunk and went to reach for my lariat on my saddle and Bob said, "You won't need that. Them colts are too young to ride!"

"I ain't gettin' my saddle, just this," I said, taking my rope off the saddle, a little perturbed. "Where's the halters?"

"They're in the barn," replied Bob. "I'll show you."

"I can find 'em," I said, not wanting to wait for Bob to get to the barn.

I found the halters in the barn hanging on a hook, and they all had lead ropes on them. The lead ropes were only about six feet long and I wanted them fifteen or twenty feet long. There were plenty. I also found a spool of soft cotton rope.

When Bob came hobbling into the barn, I asked him, "Is there any snaps here?"

"There should be some over in that box of hardware," he replied.

I went to the box and dug out a dozen snaps. I got the spool of soft cotton rope and reeled out about twenty feet of rope and cut it. I measured twelve twenty feet sections, cut them and then started to braid the snaps into one end of each section. I braided off the loose ends so they wouldn't unravel. I took the halters off the hook and replaced the lead ropes with the longer leads I'd just fixed.

I was hanging the short leads on the hook when Charlie came into the barn and asked, "What you doin'? I thought you'd be workin' on them colts."

"I'm fixin' up some equipment. I'm just about ready to start."

Charlie eyed the new lead ropes. "Remember, I need those colts halter broke by the first of September."

"They'll be ready," I said, and Charlie left.

Bob hadn't said anything during Charlie's visit. After Charlie left, he said, "This should be interesting. I don't think Charlie liked you cuttin' up his soft cotton rope."

"Apparently he'll leave a feller alone to do his work," I said.

I put the new halters over my shoulder, picked up my lariat and went to the corral. Bob followed me.

I hung the halters on the fence, opened the gate and entered the corral, lariat in hand. Bob started to follow me into the corral, but I stopped him.

"You better stay out here, old timer," I said, closing and latching the gate on him. "Things are liable to get a little western in here an' I don't want you gettin' hurt."

"But I can help," said Bob.

"I don't need any help right now," I said.

The colts ran to the far end of the corral when I entered. As I moved to the center of the corral, the colts circled around me.

I made what I was told was a hoolihan loop. I had the loop laid out on my left side and when I was ready, brought the loop around to my right, over my head and sent it toward the colt I selected. My aim was true and the loop settled over the colt's head.

When the loop settled over the colt's head, I

heard Bob shout, "Nice catch! I ain't seen a hoolihan for years!"

The colt hit the end of the rope hard and I braced for it. I needed to choke the colt down to get a halter on him. I was wishing there was a snubbing post in the middle of the corral.

Keeping a firm hold on the rope, the colt finally threw himself. I rushed up to him and before he could get up, I was on his head, holding him down.

"Throw one of them halters over here!" I shouted at Bob.

It took Bob a little time to get a halter and throw it over to me. His throw was not good and the halter landed about five feet away from me.

"Toss one over to me where I can get it!" I shouted.

Bob got another halter and threw it. It landed on the colt, causing the colt to struggle, but I managed to reach it.

I put the halter on the colt, took the lariat off his neck and, getting out of the way, I turned the colt loose.

I made another loop, picked out another colt and made a throw. Again my aim was true and I choked the colt down until he fell and I could get on his head. Bob threw another halter to me.

I haltered him and turned him loose. I repeated the procedure and soon had four colts haltered. I decided to take a little break.

Bob came over to where I was resting, staying on the outside of the corral, and said, "Where'd you learn that hoolihan? I ain't seen it for years."

"It's a pretty handy throw when ropin' horses," I said. "If a feller gets to swingin' a loop over his head too much, it tends to get the horses excited an' they'll get to runnin' too much. I think the sound of the loop cuttin' through the air spooks 'em. Besides that, I don't have much upper body strength an' I can use my body weight to throw the loop out quite a ways."

"Ever tried that underhanded throw?" asked Bob.

"Yeah," I replied. "But I ain't much good at it. I can't keep the loop open when I throw it."

"It's a good throw for catchin' horses by the front feet." said Bob.

"Yeah," I replied, wanting to drop the subject. "Too many horses get hurt when they hit the ground usin' that throw."

After a short break, I got another loop ready and caught another colt. I continued the procedure until I had four more colts caught and haltered.

I took another break and during it, Charlie came to the corral. He asked, "How you doin'?"

"I've got eight of 'em captured an' haltered," I said. "Only four more to go!"

"You've got 'em draggin' the lead ropes around," stated Charlie.

"Yep," I answered. "With them draggin' the lead ropes an' the other colts steppin' on 'em, they'll soon learn to give to the pressure. An' with them long lead ropes, it'll be easier to catch each one tomorrow."

Charlie didn't say anything and I couldn't tell if he was satisfied or not.

"You need to stick around an' watch him throw a hoolihan," said Bob. "He's pretty good!"

The last thing I needed was an audience watching me.

"It's time I caught the others," I said, making a loop in my lariat.

The colts were more nervous now and were running around me in the corral. I picked out an unhaltered colt and made my throw. At the last instant, the colt ducked his head and I missed.

"That's the first one he's missed all day!" exclaimed Bob.

Charlie was not impressed.

"That's what happens when I have an audience," I said.

Both Charlie and Bob laughed at my comment.

I made another loop, made a throw and this time my aim was good. The colt hit the end of the rope hard and I flipped the rope over on his right side and stepped in front of him. When he tried to turn away from me, I pulled hard on the slack and the colt went down. I'd tripped him.

I got to his head before he got up and held him down.

"Bob, throw me another halter!" I shouted. "On second thought, Charlie, throw me a halter. Bob's aim ain't been so good!"

"I can't throw good on these crutches!" retorted Bob.

Charlie tossed me a halter and it landed on the colt's side. I put the halter on the colt, took off my rope and turned the colt loose.

I made another loop and caught another colt. I tripped him up in the same manner I'd tripped the others. He went down a little harder and I got to him and held his head. Charlie threw me another halter; I got it on the colt and turned him loose.

I caught the two remaining colts and got halters on them. Charlie stayed until I'd haltered the last one.

When I'd let the last one go and was coiling my rope, Charlie said, "You're pretty good with that hoolihan loop."

"Twelve catches out of thirteen ain't a bad average," I said. "I like it for catchin' horses. You got a saddle horse I can use for a couple of days?"

"Yeah," replied Charlie. "What you want him for?"

"I figure I can get closer to each colt horseback, get the lead rope, dally up and give him his first lesson on bein' led. I might be draggin' some of 'em, but they'll follow another horse easier. I can get 'em close to the fence an' tie 'em each to a post. They'll get their first lesson in bein' tied."

"I've got a good, stout horse in the corral. He's well broke an' stout enough to drag any of these colts wherever you want to go. He'll do anything you ask of him an' he's as honest as the day is long."

Charlie took me over to another corral and pointed out a big bay horse. "He's the one," he said. "I'll have him caught for you after breakfast."

"I'll use my own saddle on him," I said.

"Certainly," replied Charlie.

"I'll want to use that other corral to tie the horses an' that small round corral," I said.

"Sure," said Charlie. "You goin' to leave the halters on the colts overnight?"

"Yep," I answered. "They'll be wearin' 'em all the time until they're gentle enough to walk up to."

"You appear to know what you're doin'," said Charlie.

"Halter breakin' these mustangs is a little different than breakin' a barn-raised colt that's used to seein' people. The first few days are a little rough on 'em, but things will get easier as they become accustomed to people. Today was about as rough as it'll get, unless some of 'em throw themselves while they're tied. It's all new to 'em, but they're young an' will learn fast. The trick is to keep repeatin' the lessons so they don't forget."

Charlie nodded his head in agreement.

CHAPTER 4

The next morning after breakfast, I followed Charlie to the corral where the big bay horse was that I was going to use. I'd got my halter from the car and was ready to catch the horse.

Charlie entered the corral and I followed. Before I could latch the gate, Charlie whistled and the big bay trotted over to him.

Charlie scratched the knowledge bump between the horse's ears with one hand and gave him a horse candy with the other hand.

"Now you can halter him," said Charlie.

"I never had a horse that came to me like a dog when I whistled," I said.

"The trick is like you said yesterday, repetition," said Charlie. "An' these horse treats don't hurt for reinforcement."

"You want the yearlin's to come at a whistle?" I asked.

"No, there ain't that much time. They just need to be good an' gentle."

"That's good," I said. "With these false teeth, I can't whistle!"

I haltered the horse and looked him over. He was about as structurally correct as any horse I'd seen.

"You won't need to hobble him when you saddle him," said Charlie. "He'll stand ground tied."

"He's about as good a lookin' horse as I've seen," I said.

"Yep," stated Charlie. "He's the horse I use when I go out with the boys, or irrigatin' or anything else. But, just because he's my horse, don't be easy on him. He can take anything an' he needs the work. I kinda wish we'd have kept him as a stud rather than geldin' him. He's got the right disposition."

"He's ranch-raised then," I said.

"Yep," replied Charlie. "Ranch bred, ranch born, an' ranch reared right here. Bob halter broke him as a weaner an' I put all the other trainin' on him. Be careful, he'll spin out from under you if you tell him to!"

I saddled the horse and Charlie said, "Try him out right here."

I untracked the horse, tightened the cinch and got on. I moved him out slowly then asked him to turn both directions. I didn't need to neck rein him, he responded to the leg pressure I applied. I asked him to spin and he responded, almost too good.

"This horse could win some reinin' competitions," I said.

"He's won more than one," said Charlie. "Remind me sometime an' I'll show you all the ribbons an' trophies he's won."

I was impressed. I made a mental note to have Charlie show me the awards. As I rode the horse to the corral where the yearlings were, I thought to myself, *I'm goin' to have fun ridin' this horse!*

I rode the horse to the corral and Bob was waiting for me at the gate.

"Charlie let you ride The Champ, I see," he said.

"The Champ?" I questioned. It occurred to me that I hadn't asked the horse's name.

"Yeah," replied Bob. "He's got some fancy long-winded name on his papers, but we just call him The Champ."

"He's registered?"

"Yep," answered Bob. "Every horse on this place has papers. Every horse except those rangs you're halter breakin'. Charlie must have taken a likin' to you, not everybody gets to ride that horse."

It occurred to me that I'd hired onto a pretty fancy outfit. I should have known. The road into the ranch was graded and graveled, not full of dust like on the last outfit I worked on. I had noticed that the sign said "Registered Quarter Horses and Registered Paint Horses."

"Let me in," I said. "It's time we acquainted the rangs with nobility!"

Bob opened the gate and I entered the corral. "What can I do to help?" asked Bob.

"If you want to work that other gate, I'd appreciate it. I'm goin' to catch each colt an' lead or drag him into that corral an' tie him to a post. We'll commence to teach these colts how to stand tied."

Bob started to cross the corral that the colts were in. As soon as he entered the corral, the colts started running. A man on foot in the same corral spooked all of them.

I started to tell Bob that he might be safer hobbling outside the corral, but didn't. I thought if I rode The Champ between the colts and Bob, he should be okay.

We crossed the corral without incident and all the colts were watching us warily.

"You work this gate from inside the other corral," I said. "Be sure to keep the gate between you and the colts we're puttin' in here. If you want, you can follow the colts to where they're goin' to be tied. They should follow more willingly if you're behind 'em. Don't let any of the other colts in here.

"I'll pass the lead rope around the post then tie it on the next post. I'm only goin' to leave about a foot of slack between the post an' the colt."

Bob got into position behind the gate and I reentered the corral where the colts were.

I got closer to the colts horseback before they started running. I rode up alongside one colt, grabbed the lead rope and dallied up to the saddle horn. The colt resisted being led, but I had him dallied up short so he couldn't really do anything.

I half dragged and half led the colt to the gate that Bob had opened. Inside the corral, I waited until Bob closed and latched the gate then started to the far side of the corral. Bob followed at a distance and the colt led more willingly.

I passed the lead rope around a post, went to the next post and took a couple of wraps around the post then tied it off. The Champ side-passed willingly when I needed to get close to the post.

It was interesting catching the colts. When they started running, some of them would be tripped up by another colt stepping on their lead rope and go down. At one point a colt fell right in front of The Champ, but The Champ easily jumped over him.

I was caught off guard and almost fell off, but managed to regain my balance. "You have fast reflexes," I told The Champ. "I think they're faster than mine. I'll have to stay awake!"

I'd caught half the colts and had them tied short in the corral and was taking a break when Charlie showed up. I'd loosened the cinch on The Champ.

"Seems like you're always comin' around when we're takin' a break," I said.

"No matter," said Charlie. "How's it goin'?"

"We've got about half of 'em caught an' tied," I said. "I got 'em tied real short so they can't get into any trouble. Leastways, they can't throw themselves. After we've got 'em all tied, I'll come along and tie 'em about an arm's length from the post. That's when they'll have more freedom an' learn to give to the rope. We'll be able to watch 'em real close then."

Charlie asked, "You'll have some problem givin' 'em more lead, won't you?"

"Nope," I answered. "I've got 'em tied to the next post. It'll be real easy to lengthen the lead, an' safer. Hence the long lead ropes."

Charlie looked over the situation closer. "I see," he said.

"It'll get real western catchin' the last few. They'll have more room to run, but I think The Champ an' I can handle it. Actually, it's very similar to pickin' up in the bronc ridin' at the rodeos."

Charlie just nodded his head.

"We'll give The Champ a few more minutes to rest, then continue," I said. "He's been doin' all the work!"

Charlie looked over his horse. The Champ was breathing a little heavy, but not bad. I figured the lack of a comment by Charlie signaled his approval.

We visited for a bit, then I said, "I think The Champ is rested enough. We'd better get back to work while the boss is watchin'!"

"I like it that you're takin' my horse's welfare into consideration," said Charlie.

"There's no sense in workin' him to death just because he's willin'," I said as I tightened the cinch on The Champ. "Bob's been followin' the colts to the fence once we get inside the corral. It makes it a little easier. You might want to stand clear when we come into the corral."

I got on The Champ and caught another colt, dallied up close and started to drag him to the other corral. This colt tried to bite me as we went to the corral. I had him snubbed close enough that he couldn't move his head and do me any damage.

Charlie was working the gate when we got to it and had it open. He followed the colt up to the fence. I took a wrap around the post and tied the rope at the next post.

As Charlie followed me back to the gate, I said, "That colt tried to bite me! It's a real pleasure havin' the boss help me! Doesn't happen on most outfits."

"I thought I've give Bob a break," said Charlie. "It's a little tougher on him gettin' around on crutches."

I hadn't paid much attention to Bob, but he did look tired.

"He don't really need to follow the colts to the fence, but it does make it easier on 'em," I said.

"I'll finish up for him," said Charlie.

"Don't crowd 'em, just take it easy," I said.

Charlie followed the last five colts to the fence and I got them all tied. I got off The Champ, loosened the cinch, took off the bridle, hung it over my saddle horn, and turned him loose. He just stood in the corral.

I then went to where I had each colt tied and let out their lead ropes to where there was about an arm's length from the fence. Before I gave each colt his slack, I scratched them between the ears so they could start becoming accustomed to the touch of a human. Most of them tried to pull back, but I had them tied short and they couldn't.

A few struggled tied to the fence, but there were no serious problems.

Bob hobbled along behind me trying to help but there wasn't much he could do. Charlie stood back and watched.

When I'd given each colt slack in the lead ropes, I told Bob, "We'll just let them stand an' get used to bein' tied. The smart ones will stop fightin' bein' tied pretty quick. 'Course, if one of 'em pulls back, it'll probably spook the others. Given enough time, they'll learn."

Bob agreed, then said, "You know, I was supposed to halter break these colts, but this busted leg put an end to that. I'd have done it a little different, but what you're doin' seems to be workin'."

I didn't want to hear a dissertation on how Bob would have done it, I was doing it!

"I've had some success in the past doin' this," I said.

We walked over to where Charlie was watching. "I'll probably need The Champ tomorrow. Can I use him again?"

"Sure," said Charlie. "How long you goin' to let 'em stand tied?"

"The rest of the day," I said. "I might try an' get close to some of 'em later, after they've quit fightin'.

Charlie's reply was a simple, "Okay."

"We'll keep an eye on 'em just to make sure they don't get fouled up in the leads or get a foot caught in the fence."

Charlie nodded and left. I assumed he approved.

After he left, and the colts calmed down a little, I walked inside the corral. The colts eyed me warily and a lot of them jumped forward slamming themselves into the fence. They were learning that the fence doesn't give. Some just eyed me carefully.

As I walked through the corral, I studied each colt carefully. There were all colors present, a few sorrels, a few bays, a buckskin, a palomino, a gray, and a couple of paints.

I wasn't concerned about knowing the individual sorrels and bays. They all had separate white markings on their legs and foreheads. The paints would be easy to know. The buckskin, palomino and gray were self-identifying.

Bob followed me on his crutches in the corral. When I stopped to study each colt, he stopped behind me.

"You tryin' to figure out what to name each one?" he asked.

"Nope," I replied. "Just lookin' 'em over."

"It'll be tough to name each one," said Bob.

"I ain't goin' to name 'em," I replied. "To confusin'."

"How you gonna tell 'em apart?"

"Right here," I said, pointing to my head.

I approached a few of the colts just to see what their reaction would be. They pulled back, as I expected. I did manage to get close enough to one of the sorrels, a paint, and the gray. I gently petted each one on the neck for a few minutes before I moved on. I made some mental notes on the reaction of each colt, although most were the same. They reacted out of fear. I'd have to overcome their fear of man before I could teach them to lead.

Tomorrow, I'd get close to each colt and start brushing them just to get them used to being handled by a human.

I turned the colts loose, leaving the halters on for the night. I fed them, then went to get something to eat for myself.

At supper that night, I asked Charlie, "You got a brush I can use tomorrow?"

"Yep, in the barn," he replied.

The next day, I saddled The Champ, got the brush and rode to the corral. I dropped the brush on the ground by the gate. Bob followed me on his crutches.

"We'll do it just like yesterday, Bob. You work the gate again."

"Yes sir!" was Bob's reply.

I was surprised at Bob's reply. The "sir" he added was unnecessary. I assumed he acknowledged that I was in charge of this operation.

The colts didn't appear to be as nervous as they were yesterday when I entered the corral on The Champ.

I caught each colt again by the lead rope, dallied up and started to take them into the other corral. Some of the colts needed to be dragged a little, but most followed The Champ more willingly than they did the day before. The Champ was teaching them to lead. I gave those colts that followed more willingly a little more slack in the lead.

I led them to the fence and tied them in the same manner as I did the day before.

Charlie came to the corral and gave Bob a break following the colts.

"You've got them almost broke to lead, Pete," said Charlie as he followed the colts.

"I ain't done nothin' yet," I said. "The Champ's done it all up to this point. Today we'll get 'em used to a human's touch."

"You're sayin' you're human, Pete," said Bob, smiling.

"That might be takin' a little for granted," I replied. I was grinning as I replied to Bob's comment.

When all the colts were tied short, I loosened the cinch on The Champ, hung the bridle on the saddle horn and turned him loose.

After another short visit with Charlie and Bob, I got the brush and started.

I started on the outside of the fence, petting each colt on the head and neck, then loosening the lead to about an arm's length. I talked to each colt as I brushed him. I climbed over the fence by each colt, knowing when I did, the colts would spook. But I wanted them to get used to all the actions of a human in their presence. When each colt had calmed down, I went to his head and started brushing him again. I continued talking to each colt using a soft, soothing tone of voice.

Bob stood outside the corral, constantly talking and making some comments. I was glad he made the comments, it gave me something to talk about rather than how good each colt was doing.

After the colts had found out that the brushing wasn't going to hurt them, I started brushing toward their backs. A few of the colts pulled back, then when they found out they couldn't get away, they jumped forward, slamming themselves into the fence. I needed to be careful so the colts wouldn't catch me between them and the fence.

As I considered this possibility, I smiled and thought, *That might hurt!*

After I'd brushed each colt as far back on his back as he'd let me, I'd brush under his belly, then go to the off side and start brushing from that side. A horse needs to be taught everything from both sides.

A few of the colts got a little more nervous when I approached from the right side, but with some gentle handling from that side, they soon calmed down.

When I had each colt brushed on both sides, I decided to see if they would lead without The Champ in front of them. I untied the lead rope of one colt from the far post and, keeping the rope around the post closest to the colt, approached him. He backed up a little, but I kept him close to the post. I started brushing him and he stood still. Slowly, I took the lead from around the post. The colt was basically free now, I was the only thing holding him. I continued brushing him, pulling him slightly toward me. He turned toward me and I soon had him facing the center of the corral. There was no corral fence in front of him; his rump was pointed toward the fence.

I tossed the brush to the side of him and he jumped away from it, but I held him and he stopped.

I continued to talk to the colt. "Let's see if you can lead," I said, as I gave the lead rope a slight tug.

The colt took a step forward, then stopped, not knowing what was expected of him.

"That's good!" I said. "That's what we want!" I gave him a pat on the neck and scratched him between the ears.

I gave the lead rope another tug and the colt stepped forward again. Slowly the colt moved forward. I walked away, holding the lead rope. Hesitantly, the colt followed. Soon the colt was following me. He was starting to lead. He balked a few times, but a firm tug on the lead rope convinced him to follow.

I led him around for about fifteen minutes, then took him back to the fence and tied him to it, telling him what a good colt he was.

I went to the next colt and repeated the procedure with him, with similar results, spending about the same amount of time with him.

The third colt, the gray, gave me more difficulty. When I had him facing the center of the corral, I gave a tug on the lead rope and he backed up into the fence. When his rump hit the fence, he jumped forward almost hitting me, but I stepped out of his way.

He ran past me, but I held the rope and stopped him.

"That's kinda what we want," I said, as I approached the colt. "But not exactly."

I petted the colt and soon had him calmed down. I gave the colt a tug on the lead rope again, and he tried to run past me.

"You're a little too willin', Little Ghost Horse," I said. Without knowing it, I'd named the gray.

I spent more time with the gray colt than the other two, but finally had him following me. He still tried to pass me if Bob said something or a slight breeze kicked up some dust, but I held him. When I had him following me reasonably well, I took him back to the fence and tied him.

"You're goin' to take more time, Little Ghost Horse," I said. I moved on to the next colt.

I repeated the same procedure on the next couple of colts with about the same results. When I had about half the colts led around, I stopped for dinner.

At dinner, I met Charlie. He asked, "How's it goin?"

"I've led about half the colts around," I said.

"You haven't got kicked or knocked down yet?" asked Charlie.

"Not yet," I replied. "But I still got half of 'em to go."

"I've been kinda busy this mornin'," said Charlie. "But I'll be down this afternoon to watch how you're doin'."

"Come down any time," I said.

After dinner, I started the same procedure with the remaining colts. One of the paints didn't want to lead so I looped the end of the lead rope over his rump and gave it a tug. The colt jumped forward, then stopped. I tugged again on the lead rope and the rope over his rump at the same time and the colt jumped forward again and stopped.

Charlie showed up while I was working the paint.

"A little reluctant, is he?"

"Yep," I replied. "It's a start an' stop situation. We'll keep after it until he's convinced he needs to move forward."

I continued using the tug on the lead rope and the tug on the rump rope until the colt started to follow.

"Progress is kinda slow on colts this age," I said. "A lot of repetition is needed."

"Yes," said Charlie.

I led the remaining colts around about fifteen minutes each. When I finished with the last one, I led each one into the bigger corral and turned them loose, leaving the halters and lead ropes on. Then I fed the colts.

I led The Champ back to the barn and unsaddled him. "I don't think we'll be needin' you tomorrow," I said, somewhat regretfully. I liked riding the horse and had rarely ridden a horse so well trained.

The next day, I caught the colts by the lead ropes and tied them to the fence. Some of the colts needed the rump rope to be led to the fence, and after some convincing, I had them all tied. I went to brushing each colt as I had done previously, then led them around the corral. I brushed them on both sides and down on their legs toward their feet. Some of the colts tried to kick me as I brushed their hind feet, but I had my free hand on their rump and pushed them away.

I did get a glancing blow or two from some of them, but pushing them away caused them to have to regain their balance. Their attempts to kick me were, for the most part, unsuccessful.

CHAPTER 5

Later that afternoon, Charlie showed up with a visitor. I could tell from his hat and the insignia on his shirt that he was from the BLM.

"Pete, this is Claude Harrison. Claude's in charge of the BLM out here. Claude, this is Pete Peterson. He's taken over halter breakin' these colts since Bob broke his leg."

When the introductions were over, Claude asked me, "How are you doing with the colts?"

"The colts are comin' along just fine," I answered. "Some of 'em are a little slow, but that's to be expected at their age. We'll spend a little more time with 'em. I've worked a little more than half of 'em today, still got the rest to go. You can watch if you want to."

"I'd like to if you don't mind," said the BLM director. Claude climbed up on the fence and Charlie stood beside him.

The first colt I started to work after Claude

showed up was a little reluctant to lead. I looped the long end of the lead rope over his rump and gave a tug.

The colt jumped forward and almost knocked me down. I didn't go all the way down, just to my knees. I held onto the lead rope and the colt stopped.

"You okay?" hollered Bob.

I looked over at Charlie as I got up. He was laughing. Claude had a look of surprise on his face.

"I'm okay," I said as I got up, brushing the dirt off my pants. "This colt is a little too anxious to learn! He did better yesterday."

I gave the lead rope a slight tug and the colt stepped forward toward me. Another tug and he stepped closer. I started to back up, applying a little pressure on the lead and the colt followed. I led the colt up to where Claude was sitting on the fence.

I asked Claude, "You wanna lead him?"

"No!" answered Claude adamantly.

I led the other colts around, following the same procedure without much trouble. Sometime during the day, Claude and Charlie left. I didn't see them go, I was busy.

After a couple of days working the colts the

same way each day, they were following me on a loose lead rope. At this point, they would have been considered halter broke by most people. I could walk up behind them by putting a hand on their rumps. As long as they knew I was there I wouldn't get kicked. I talked constantly to the colts when I was around them. But I wasn't done. I still needed to sack them out.

Bob said, "Them colts are pretty well broke now. They follow you around like a puppy. An' it didn't take near as long as I figured it would!"

"I've still got some more to do," I said.

"Like what?"

"I've got to pick up each one's feet an' sack 'em out."

One morning, I took an old saddle blanket from the barn and after I'd tied each colt to the fence, I walked through the middle of the corral, waving it over my head and all around. The colts naturally spooked when I did this and a lot of them pulled back trying to get away from the flying blanket.

"You've got 'em all so as they stand tied good an' now you're tryin' to spook 'em back to what they were," said Bob. "What's goin' on?"

"Just part of their trainin'," I said. "They

need to know that everything a man does ain't goin' to hurt 'em."

After I'd walked around the colts for a time waving the saddle blanket and they'd settled down, I approached each colt and slapped the blanket on each one, from his head to his rump. This caused some of them a lot of fright and they tried to get away, but couldn't. Soon they found out that the blanket wasn't going to hurt them and settled down.

I untied each colt, took him to the middle of the corral and threw the blanket at him. A few of the colts still tried to get away but I held them. I repeated this action until each colt learned that the blanket wasn't going to hurt them.

A day of this procedure and they were all pretty much accustomed to the blanket being tossed at them. I was pleased with the results.

I repeated the procedure with each colt every day. Then I started picking up each colt's feet. I'd start with the left front foot, pick it up and just hold it a minute or two then set it down. Then I'd pick up the colt's left rear foot and hold it a minute or two and set it down. I made sure I brought the rear foot forward before stretching it out behind him. Some of the colts were real touchy about having their hind feet picked up, but I persisted. Some tried to kick me, but I pushed them away with my free hand. I did get kicked a time or two, and it hurt. But it didn't hurt bad enough to stop. I could walk it off.

Charlie watched this and nodded his approval.

I repeated this procedure for a few days and soon had each colt where I could pick up all four feet without difficulty.

One morning after breakfast, I asked Charlie, "You got an old saddle I can use?"

Charlie gave me a surprised look and said, "There's one in the barn. I'll get it for you. What do you want it for?"

"It's part of the colt's continuing education. I'm goin' to saddle each colt an' get him used to bein' saddled. It'll make it easier when the colts are big enough to ride."

I went to the barn with Charlie and he pointed to a saddle on a rack. "That one ain't bein' used, take it."

I took the saddle to the corral and dropped it unceremoniously in front of a colt. He jumped away from it and eyed it suspiciously. I picked up the saddle, held it in front of the colt to smell then put it on his back. The colt tried to jump away from it, but I held it on his back.

When the colt stopped jumping, I took it off and threw it back on. I repeated this until the colt didn't even flinch when I put the saddle on. Then I did the same from the right side. A few soothing words of praise helped ease the situation for the colt.

When the colt didn't move when I put the saddle on from either side, I adjusted the off billet to fit the colt, threw the saddle on and cinched it up. I didn't cinch it tight, just enough to keep the saddle in place.

When the cinch was tightened, the colt jumped forward. This was new and unexpected for him! I gave a tug on the lead rope and the colt jumped forward again. He didn't know what I wanted with the saddle on.

A few more jumps after gentle tugs on the lead and the colt was walking. He'd found out that the saddle wasn't going to harm him. A few more words of praise helped the situation.

I repeated the procedure with each colt. Some of the colts needed more work with this and I gave it to them.

I spent the next few days repeating the procedure from the beginning. I'd taken the long lead ropes off the halters and replaced them with the shorter leads. I'd catch each colt, halter him, tie him to the fence, sack him out with the saddle blanket, pick up all four feet, saddle him and lead him around.

After breakfast one morning, I asked Charlie if there was a horse trailer I could use.

"Yep," replied Charlie.

"Can you have someone park it near the corral?"

"I'll do it myself," answered Charlie. "You goin' to load the colts?"

"That's about the last lesson to be taught. A couple of days of loadin' 'em an' I figure I'll be done. Then they'll all be halter broke. I can't think of anythin' else that needs to be taught. Give me a couple of days of loadin' 'em then come down an' watch. You can even have the BLM guy come, if you want."

"Claude will be here when the BLM picks up the colts, the first of September," said Charlie. "That's only four days away."

"They should be ready by then," I said.

I spent the next few days loading the colts and unloading them in the trailer. A few needed the rump rope to be convinced they needed to go in the trailer, but after a time, I had them jumping in freely.

The first of September came and the BLM

showed up with two twenty-foot gooseneck trailers. They also brought twelve halters and lead ropes.

Charlie brought Claude over to me.

"Are the colts halter broke?" asked Claude.

"Yep," I answered. "They're broke to lead, you can pick up all four feet on all …"

"At the same time?" interrupted Claude, with a smile on his face.

Charlie and I both laughed.

"If you want," I answered. "It's suggested you pick 'em up one at a time. You can saddle 'em up an' they'll load in the trailer."

"Show me," said Claude.

I took a halter Claude offered, walked into the corral and caught a colt. I led the colt to the fence where I'd left the saddle the night before, saddled him and led him around. I picked up all four feet, led the colt around, unsaddled him and loaded him in the BLM trailer.

I went back to where Charlie and Claude were standing. "They're all pretty much the same," I said. I couldn't tell if Claude was impressed or not.

"If they're pretty much all the same, just load them up," said Claude.

"They're all the same," said Charlie.

I caught another colt and led him to a BLM ranger to load.

"Be gentle," I said. "Them colts ain't been abused."

I watched the ranger load the colt, then caught another one. All the colts loaded easily. Claude watched, but didn't say anything.

When the last colt was loaded, the ranger told me, "You've done a good job on those colts. When I unloaded them, the only time they'd ever been handled was when they were freeze branded. I'm impressed."

"That's good," I said. "What does your boss think of 'em?"

"It's hard to say what Claude thinks," said the ranger. "He's pretty tight-mouthed."

With the last colt loaded, Claude told Charlie, "I'll be sending you a check after the auction. Let's go, Harry."

The BLM trucks left and I went to Charlie. "I guess I'm done here," I said.

"You can stay until after the BLM sale if you want," said Charlie. "It's day after tomorrow."

"I won't have nothin' to do tomorrow," I said.

"If you want, you can ride out with me an' check the cows. I've been a little lax on that lately."

I asked, "Will we see any of your stud bunches?"

"It's possible we might see the paint horses. They ain't too far away," replied Charlie.

"I'll do that," I said.

The next morning I went with Charlie. As he saddled The Champ he said, "You can ride that paint horse. He's well broke."

I saddled the paint, regretting that I couldn't ride The Champ. But I couldn't expect the boss to let me ride his horse when I was going out riding with him.

The paint horse was well broke and I liked riding him.

As we rode out to check the cattle, Charlie said, "You've done a good job with the mustangs, I'm pleased."

I accepted the compliment and said, "It took a lot of foot work an' repetition. I was startin' to get a little bored. I'm glad to be horseback again. I was beginnin' to wonder when I was goin' to be on a horse again. This horse appears to be about as well broke as The Champ."

"He does good," stated Charlie. "He's a little headstrong an' I had a time trainin' him. But he's good."

We rode through little bunches of cattle and all seemed well. When Charlie was satisfied his cattle were okay, he said, "Let's go over this way. We might see the paint horse bunch."

We came to a gate and Charlie opened it. I felt a little foolish, the boss was opening the gate for me!

I rode through it, Charlie closed the gate and we went on.

When we topped a little rise, Charlie stopped. "They're over there," he said.

I'd been looking for horses, but looking in the wrong direction.

Below us in a little valley was the stud bunch. I could see about twenty mares and it appeared that most of them had colts. There was a lot of color.

"We don't want to get to close to 'em," said Charlie. "The stud doesn't have any fear of man an' he'll come out to meet us. Look 'em over from here."

"There's a lot of color down there," I said. "A lot of money, also."

"Yep," answered Charlie. "Bob will halter break the colts when we wean 'em sometime in October. He'll have an easier time of it than you did with the mustangs. The mothers are all halter broke an' they'll learn to lead followin' their moms."

Charlie got a rough count on the horses and asked, "Seen enough?"

"Yep," I answered.

We headed back to the ranch, unsaddled our horses and went to the house.

"I'll have a check for you after breakfast in the mornin'," said Charlie.

I put my saddle in the car and went to the bunkhouse and started to gather up my belongings. I was going to leave in the morning and wanted to have everything except my bedroll and shaving gear loaded. I did some laundry and when it was done, I set out some clean clothes for tomorrow.

Bob was there and asked, "Packin' up, are you?"

"Yep. It's time to move on."

"I was sorta hopin' you'd stick around an' help me halter break the weaners," he said.

"There ain't nothin' for me to do around here till the colts are ready to be weaned, an' Charlie didn't say nothin' about it when we were out checkin' the cattle." I said. "I need a little more action."

"I learned a lot tryin' to help you," said Bob.

"I appreciate it," I said. "Thanks for your help." I thanked Bob even though he didn't help much, but he did try, in spite of his broken leg. One thing he did do was talk constantly and that talking helped get the colts used to man.

"I never would have thought of the long lead ropes on the halters!" said Bob. "I was wonderin' how you'd handle that an' you seemed to handle it okay."

"Yep," I said. "Let's get some supper!"

We went to eat and Bob talked to Charlie constantly about how good a job I'd done with the colts. I got the impression he was trying to talk Charlie into keeping me on. While that was kind on Bob's part, I really wanted to move on and get a riding job somewhere.

Finally, Charlie asked, "Do you want to stay on an' help Bob with the colts? You can if you want."

"I appreciate the offer, Charlie," I said, "But I'd best be movin' on an' lookin' for a ridin' job somewheres. I might get on helpin' out with the fall gather."

When I said that, Charlie started to name some ranches that might be hiring. When he named the last outfit I worked for, I smiled.

"You know that outfit?" he asked.

"Yep," I answered. "I worked for 'em for one

day. The boss, I never did know his name, he rolled ..."

"Howard Wells," interrupted Charlie.

"Well," I continued, "he's a drunk. He rolled the truck an' George ended up takin' him to the hospital. I met George at a steakhouse an' told him I was done an' didn't want to play nursemaid to a drunk. I didn't even wait for a check. I never mentioned workin' for 'em 'cause I didn't think it would help me get on here."

"You were right! George Cooper. Is he still there?"

"He was when I left," I said.

"He's been there a long time," said Charlie. "There's some sort of family ties there."

"I won't go back there to work." I said.

"That's too bad. George could use the help."

"He's got Davy helpin' him," I said.

"They'll be all right then," said Charlie.

Charlie named off some ranches where he thought I might get hired, then said, "You can use my name as a reference if you want. I'll give you a good one."

I thanked Charlie and asked for directions to the ranches he'd named.

"I'll have a written list of directions for you in the mornin'," said Charlie.

"Good," I said. "Well, it's past my bedtime." I left and went to the bunkhouse. I slept good that night, not knowing where I was going or what I'd be doing the next day.

CHAPTER 6

The next morning I shaved, put on my clean clothes and put my bedroll in the car. After breakfast, Charlie had a check for me, a ranch advertisement, and a list of ranches and directions to each one. He'd also written down the names of the person I should contact at each ranch. He'd also included a handwritten recommendation. I looked over the list and thanked Charlie. Then I looked at my check. I was surprised!

"This check is almost double what you said you were payin'!" I said.

"I told you there'd be a bonus if you did a good job an' Claude told me to take good care of you. He said he might have more mustangs to break next year an' would like you to do it. Are you interested?"

"I don't know where I'll be next year an' hate to commit that far in the future," I said.

"I understand. The ranch phone number is

on our flyer. You call if you need a job the last part of July or the first part of August. You can cash that check in town."

I shook hands with Charlie and Bob and went to the car. As I walked away, I heard Charlie say, "I can write a check for a smaller amount if you want!"

I turned around and saw Charlie grinning on the porch.

"I'd hate to cause you more work!" I said.

I left the ranch with Charlie smiling. I was too.

I drove into town and cashed the check, then bought some new clothes. I was at a loss at what direction to go. The list Charlie had given me was complete, but the ranches on it were scattered. Some of them were more than a hundred miles away.

I decided I'd go north, looking for work. It was a little early to get hired on for the fall gather, but I might find an outfit that was shorthanded. The first outfit I went to had plenty of help and I drove on.

The second ranch also had all the help they needed and I went farther. The third ranch wanted someone to help pick up the rest of the hay, but I'd spent a lot of time on my feet and wasn't interested.

The day was fast winding down and I considered whether or not go to the next town and get a motel room or camp out. I decided to go to town. I didn't have any groceries or anything to cook with and was getting kinda hungry. I could eat at a café and spend the night in a motel.

The following morning, with renewed vigor, I set out to find a job. I wasn't getting too concerned, I still had plenty of money and plenty of time. It was still early to start the fall gather.

The first ranch I stopped at wasn't looking for any help so I drove on. At the second ranch, two cowboys were driving out. We visited for a while and one of the cowboys informed me that they were quitting.

"How come?" I asked.

"He ain't got no money to pay us," I was told. "He owes us a month's wage an' we figured it was best to get out before he ended up owin' us a whole bunch. If you're lookin' to get hired on, you might be better to look somewhere else."

"How come he ain't got no money?" I asked.

"He says his wife's in the hospital, but we don't believe him," said the driver of the car.

"He's got money," said the passenger in the car. "He's just an old miser an' don't want to part with his cash!"

"Thanks," I said. "Maybe I'd best move on."

"Oh, he's lookin' for help all right," said the driver. "We were the only help he had, so now he don't have nobody. You can get hired on, if you want to work for free."

The car drove off, headed toward the town I'd just left. I considered getting back on the road and going to the next ranch, but was curious about this place. The two cowboys that I'd met hadn't impressed me. I wanted more information, so I drove onto the ranch and up to the ranch house. I parked the car and walked up to the house and knocked on the door. There was no reply in the house.

I turned to leave and saw someone coming from the barn. "Hello!" he said.

"Howdy," I replied.

The man was elderly and walked with a limp. His wrinkled, deeply suntanned face indicated he'd spent a lot of time outside.

"What you lookin' for?" he asked.

"I was lookin' for the ranch owner or foreman," I replied.

"That's me," he said. "On both counts."

"Good," I said. "The fellers that I met comin' in said you might be lookin' for some help."

"Them two good for nothin' drifters just quit

me!" said the owner. "They weren't much good, goin' off to town every night an' gettin' drunk! They were the only help I had an' they weren't much help at that!"

"Well," I said, reaching for the letter of recommendation Charlie had given me. "I'm lookin for a ridin' job." I kinda took offense at his description of the two fellers that had just quit. *I* am a drifter!

I handed the letter to the owner and he read it over carefully.

"So, you worked for Charlie, huh?"

"Yeah, I halter broke some mustang colts for him."

"Charlie's a good man," said the owner. "I've bought most all my horses from him an' they're well broke! He knows how to break an' train horses. I'm gettin' a little too old an' stove up to do it myself any more. I don't have any colts to break."

"I was lookin' to hire on for the fall gather," I said.

"There ain't much to gather here," said the owner. "I only got a few hundred head, but they're up high an' it's rough country. I could use you, but can't pay until I sell the calves. My wife's in the hospital an' the bills are mountin' up."

"The two fellers that left said you were havin' some financial troubles an' said that your wife was in the hospital."

The owner told me about his wife's problems and it sounded pretty serious.

When he finished, he said, "Oh, by the way, I'm Dennis Jorgensen."

He stuck out his hand with the letter from Charlie.

I took the letter and shook his hand. "I'm Pete Peterson," I said.

"Glad to know you," said Dennis. "Like I said, I can use you, but I can't pay until after the calves are sold. The wife an' me used to do everything ourselves, then she started feelin' poorly an' I had to hire some temporary help, just to get through the busy times. I've been doin' everything, from irrigatin' to brandin' to cookin'. It's been a little rough. Sometimes I've got some good help, other times it's been poor help, like them two drifters that just left. They weren't no good!"

"Well," I said, "I'm good till after the fall gather. I'm sort of a drifter myself."

"Why don't you settle down, light in one spot?" asked Dennis.

"I kinda like seein' some new country, meetin'

some new folks an' seein' how other ranches do things. I ain't ready."

"I know the feelin'," said Dennis.

We visited for a while and I told Dennis about some of the ranches I'd worked on.

"You ever work for Howard Wells?" asked Dennis.

"Yeah," I said. "But I wasn't goin' to tell you about that. It ain't really a good place to work. I only spent one day there. Didn't like workin' for a drunk."

I was thinking that all these ranchers knew each other.

"I heard that Howard rolled his truck an' ended up in the hospital. I heard he died," said Dennis.

"I was there when he rolled the truck, but didn't see it. I hadn't heard he'd died."

"It wasn't the accident that killed him," said Dennis. "It was the alcohol. I heard that he had enough in his system that he should have been dead when he got to the hospital."

"I guess that's too bad," I said. I really didn't care one way or the other.

"You can put your bedroll in the bunkhouse, your saddle in the barn, an' I'll show you around a little.

I put my bedroll in the bunkhouse, which was simple. A wood-burning stove for heat, a table and a couple of chairs, a couple of bunks and a bathroom with a shower. There were some empty beer cans scattered around and an accumulation of dust on everything. I figured I could have the place cleaned up in an hour.

I got my saddle from the car and met Dennis on my way to the barn with it.

"I haven't been in the bunkhouse," said Dennis. "Is it livable?"

"I can have it suitable in about an hour," I said. "Some dirt an' some empty beer cans. It won't take much."

"Good," said Dennis. "I never should have hired them guys. They weren't no good. Just a couple of drunks! Put your saddle on one of them empty racks an' I'll show you our horses."

I put my saddle on a rack and looked around the tack room in the barn. It was small, but neat and clean.

"That's my wife's saddle," said Dennis, taking the pad and blanket off it. "She ain't used it much for the last year. Been sickly."

I looked at the saddle. It was clean and well oiled.

"Looks like you've took good care of it," I said.

"Yep, sometimes I ain't got much to do an' I can stay busy keepin' things in shape. But that ain't often. Come out an' I'll show you the horses you can use."

I followed Dennis out to the horse pen. There were six horses in the pen and they were all in good shape.

"You can use the three bays," said Dennis. "They all come from Charlie an' they're all well broke. My wife used 'em. I use the black, the paint, an' the buckskin. The paint an' the buckskin come from Charlie. I broke the black, probably the last horse I'll ever break. All the horses that come from Charlie got papers, but that don't mean much to me. Can't ride papers. While we're here we might just as well feed 'em. Grab a bale an' put it in that feeder. I'll put another one in here."

I did as I was told and as I left the corral, I ran my hand over the horse's rumps, talking to them.

Dennis told me a little about the horses I was assigned to ride. "There ain't a flaw in any of 'em," he said.

"Are they broke as good as the horse Charlie calls The Champ?" I asked.

"Almost," replied Dennis. "Did Charlie let you ride The Champ?"

"Yep," I replied. "He's about the best trained horse I ever rode."

"Then Charlie must have taken a liken to you. That horse has won just about everythin' in a three or four state area around here."

"I saw all the trophies an' awards he's won," I said.

Then Dennis told me about the three horses he rode. He was mighty proud of the black and spent a lot of time telling me his history. I thought Dennis got to bragging a little when he talked about the black.

"Tomorrow, we'll saddle up an' I'll show you a little about the place. You just take it easy the rest of the afternoon. I'll fix supper an' we'll eat about six in the house. My cookin' ain't the best, but I ain't made myself sick eatin' it. After supper, you can watch TV in the house if you want. I like to catch up on the news every day."

"I could watch the news," I said, "but I ain't interested in anything else."

"Whatever," said Dennis. "Come to the house about six."

I went to the bunkhouse and started to clean it up then went to the house for supper.

Supper wasn't bad. I've sure eaten a lot worse on some of the outfits I've worked on.

Dennis told me, "Breakfast will be at six in the mornin'. Don't be late or you won't get anythin'."

I laughed. "I won't be late."

I went to bed after supper, looking forward to riding the horses Dennis had got from Charlie.

CHAPTER 7

After breakfast the next morning, we went to the horse pen.

I asked, "Any particular bay I should ride today?"

"The bally-faced bay was ridden the day before yesterday an' the bay with the socks was ridden the day before that," said Dennis. "Take the solid bay."

I haltered the solid bay and started to saddle him. I was putting hobbles on the horse and Dennis stopped me.

"You don't need to hobble these horses when you saddle 'em. Charlie broke 'em."

"Okay," I said. I put the hobbles back on the saddle and saddled the horse. I noticed Dennis watching me as he saddled his horse. He was taking my measure.

I untracked the horse and got on. Dennis was already on his horse, the black.

"You ready?" he asked.

"Ready for anythin'," I answered.

We started out at a fast walk.

"What do you call this horse?" I asked.

"That's the wife's horse. She likes bays an' calls him Bay Boy. The bally-faced bay she calls Sparkle an' the other one she calls Socks. They're all good horses."

I laughed a little. Every outfit has a horse called Socks.

We rode through hay fields. The hay was already hauled off except for a couple of broken bales. There was new growth starting.

"I was goin' to gather up the broken bales today, but I can get them day after tomorrow. I'm goin' to go to town tomorrow an' visit the wife, but I figure I ought to show you the lay of the land. I was goin' to stay in town with her, but she convinced me there was too much to do out here, so I go visit her once a week. In a lot of ways, she's really my boss, but she's generally right."

I laughed.

"That's only one of the reasons I'm not married," I said. "I sorta like bein' my own boss."

Dennis laughed. "That'll change if you get married. But the misses an' I generally agree on what has to be done. Of course, if she'd have been here when I hired them two bums, she'd never have let me hire 'em. We've partnered up on this place for the past thirty-some odd years an' even though it's a small operation compared to the others in the area, we seem to do all right."

We came to a wire gate and I said, "I'll get it."

"No need," said Dennis. He rode up to the gate, opened it from horseback and rode through it. I watched in amazement. I'd never seen a man open a wire gate from horseback and ride through it.

"Come on!" said Dennis.

I rode through the opening and Dennis closed the gate.

"I always had to get off an' open wire gates," I said.

"When you get older, you start findin' easy ways to do things," he said. "You can do that horseback on any of my horses."

"I'll remember that," I said. "But I won't wait till I get older, I'll start doin' it today. I'll only be a little older then!"

Dennis smiled. "This is the main gate onto the property from this end of the ranch. We'll be bringin' the cattle through it from the mountain. We'll turn 'em loose on the hay field."

We rode to the south until we came to a ditch.

"I dug this ditch from the river. I was just goin' to come out an' start diggin' but the wife convinced me to hire a surveyor to come out an' plot it. I'm glad she did 'cause I never would have dug it this way. That was more than thirty years ago an' even today the ditch looks like it's goin' uphill. But water runs down it."

"An optical illusion," I said.

"I guess that's what they call it."

"It looks like it runs uphill to me," I said.

"I can irrigate all the hay fields from this ditch. I built a diversion dam in the river an' can regulate how much water I want. I own most all the water rights from the river an' sell some water to the neighbors downstream."

"You didn't dig this ditch by hand, did you?"

"No," replied Dennis. "I bought a ditcher an' dug it with that. I still use it to clean the ditch every year."

We rode farther south until we came to another fence.

"I'll get this gate," I said, anxious to see if I could open a wire gate and ride through it.

"You feel like you're already gettin' older?" asked Dennis.

I smiled. "I'm already about a half hour older than I was!"

Dennis laughed. "Don't drop the gate or you'll have to get off to get it!"

"I'm aware of that!" I said.

I went to the gate and opened it horseback. I found Bay Boy was very responsive to the cues I gave him with my legs. I wasn't able to test the horse as to his responsiveness just riding at a walk to this point. I was pleased.

I held the gate open for Dennis and he rode through it. I closed the gate feeling very satisfied with myself and the horse.

"This is a little holdin' pasture, just a couple of acres," said Dennis. "The first day we gather, we'll leave all the gates open an' the cows can go straight to the hay fields. The second day we'll have to close the gates so the cattle don't come back lookin' for a calf or whatever.

"This holdin' pasture was another one of the wife's ideas an' it works good. If we hadn't have put it in, we'd have had to hire an extra man just to open the gate into the hay field."

"Your wife seems to have some good ideas on how to operate this place," I said.

"Yeah," said Dennis after some thought. "But I'd have thought of it eventually. She's always one jump ahead of me."

We rode through the holding pasture. I opened the gate on the far side.

"You can just leave that gate open," said Dennis. "We'll be comin' back through it."

Rather than just dropping the gate post, I took it all the way back to the fence and propped it up against the fence. "I'll just leave it standin' up then I don't have to get off to close it," I said.

Dennis nodded his approval as I did.

"This is BLM ground we're on now," said Dennis. "It stretches for a few hundred yards or so through here. I been tryin' to buy it or trade it from the BLM but ain't been successful. It's just waste ground. I figured I could winter some cows on it. My neighbor, Jack, borders this BLM ground on the west. His house is a couple of miles to the west. He sometimes comes out to help us when we gather. The Forest Service ground borders the BLM ground on the south end."

"Seems like this little stretch of ground would be difficult for the BLM to manage," I said.

"They don't manage it," said Dennis. "It just sticks up through here like a sore thumb. It ain't even fenced on the Forest Service boundary."

The brush was thicker on the BLM ground and some of the sagebrush was five or six feet tall. There was a narrow trail through the brush and I followed Dennis through it.

Soon we came to a large creek. It was almost a river. Then we got to a man-made dam.

"This is the diversion dam I made years ago. We cross all the cattle below the dam. It gets pretty muddy above the dam. I put a few dump truck loads of gravel in below the dam an' the footin' is better. We had a few cows bog down when we crossed above it. The wife had some trouble with her horse tryin' to get a cow free one year. She ended up soakin' wet. That's when she convinced me to put in the gravel below the dam. A few hundred cows crossin' the creek tends to loosen up the bottom."

"Was she ridin' one of the horses you got from Charlie?" I asked.

"No," answered Dennis. "She was ridin' a horse I broke for her. He got pretty old an' I retired him. We found him a year later. He died in one of the hay fields. He was a good old horse."

We rode up the river on the east side.

"We'll bring most of the cattle to the holdin' pasture on the west side of the river. We'll lock 'em in there, then come back an' ride this side of the river."

"River!" I said. "This ain't much more than a big creek!"

"In this country, where there ain't much water, it's a river!" said Dennis. "All the little streams empty into it from each one of the canyons. Some of the springs in the canyons have probably dried up by now. There might be some pools of water left in a few spots in each canyon. We'll have to ride each canyon to get all the cattle. If we don't find any cattle in a canyon, we'll have to come back to the mouth of the canyon an' go to the next one. It gets pretty steep toward the top an' there's a lot of shale. Can't ride a horse across it!"

"Sounds like pretty rough country," I said.

"It is," said Dennis. "You'll find out how rough when we start gatherin'."

We rode for a few more miles and Dennis told me about each canyon as we came to it. He indicated that there were some big meadows in some of the canyons and they provided a lot of feed. In some canyons there wasn't much feed and the entrances were pretty narrow. In a few spots the cattle would have to come through in single file. Dennis knew this country like the back of his hand, and I mentioned this to him.

"I been runnin' cows here for better than

thirty years an' been over every inch of it!" he said. "I got in a few jackpots when I tried to go somewhere where's I couldn't."

Jokingly, I asked, "Did you have much trouble with the Indians when you came into the country?"

Dennis looked at me in surprise. He saw that I was smiling when I said that and he smiled.

"I ain't that old!" he said. "The Indian problems had all been solved when I got to the country. But I have found a few arrowheads in the area. When you meet Jack, you ask him about the Indians. He's full-blooded."

We rode on for a few more miles then Dennis said, "It's time we headed back. Supper will be late by the time we get back an' feed an' I fix it."

"I'll feed if you want to fix supper," I said.

We rode back the same way we'd come and as we rode past the mouth of each canyon, I tried to remember what Dennis had told me about each one. It was tough, I had too much information.

When we got to the holding pasture, Dennis said, "I got the gate."

He closed it, without getting off the black horse.

We rode to the hay field and Dennis said, "I got the gate."

"I can get it," I said.

"Nope," said Dennis. "I like to keep my horse in trainin' as much as possible."

I smiled. I'd never been on an outfit where there was almost an argument over who was going to open or close a gate. I'd been on plenty of outfits where there was an argument about that, but on this place, everyone wanted to do it! On other outfits, nobody wanted to!

As we rode through the hay field, I noticed the broken bales we'd passed earlier.

"You're goin' to town tomorrow, right?" I asked.

"That's the plan," answered Dennis.

"If you give me the keys to the pickup, I'll come out an' gather up those broken bales tomorrow mornin'."

"You'll do that?" Dennis seemed amazed.

"Yep, unless you've got somethin' else," I said.

"The keys are in the truck," said Dennis. "I don't have anythin' else for you to do tomorrow. I thought you might want to go to town with me."

"Nope," I said. "I just come from town. Don't need any more of it."

Dennis looked a little more surprised.

"I'll throw those broken bales to the horses,"

I said. "No sense in wastin' it. There should be a couple of day's feed there."

"Just feed 'em enough to keep 'em. They're gettin' too fat as it is," said Dennis.

We got to the barn and I volunteered to unsaddle Dennis's horse while he fixed supper.

"Nope," he said. "I always take care of my own horse an' equipment. You gettin' kinda hungry? You ain't had no dinner."

"I'm used to goin' without a noon meal," I said.

I fed the horses and went to the bunkhouse to get cleaned up. Then I went to the house.

"A few more minutes an' supper will be ready," said Dennis. "Get yourself a cup of coffee an' sit down."

I did as I was told and soon was eating supper. When done, I volunteered to help with the dishes.

"If you really want to help with the dishes, just scrape 'em off an' put 'em in the dishwasher," said Dennis. "That was a surprise I got for the wife some years ago an' she sure appreciated it. It was tough on her, ridin' all day, takin' care of her horse, fixin' supper then doin' the dishes. I had a rough time plumbin' it in here, but finally got it. She had a little more free time after I got it workin'."

"Sounds like your wife did a lot of things around here," I said. "Maybe even to the point of replacin' a hired hand or two."

"Yep," said Dennis. "She's worth her weight in gold. Even more, she don't weigh much!"

"I'd certainly like to meet her," I said.

"You will when I can get her out of the hospital. When she gets home, she won't be able to do much. You make a good impression on her an' she might continue lettin' you ride her horses!"

I smiled. "I'll try."

"Tomorrow, while I'm in town, you pick up that hay like you said you'd do. There ain't nothin' else to do, you can just loaf around till I get back. You can fix yourself anythin' you want for your noon meal. Everything you need is in the kitchen."

"I thought I'd saddle another horse an' see some more of the country," I said.

"Like to stay busy, huh?"

"Yep," I replied.

CHAPTER 8

The next day after breakfast, Dennis went to town. I got the pickup and a pitchfork and drove out in the hay field. I got the broken bales, fed half of it to the horses and left the other half on the truck.

I saddled the bay horse called Sparkle and rode out on the hay fields. I tried to envision what the layout was from the air. It seemed very organized on the ground.

The irrigation ditches were all well maintained and I got to a pond that collected the overflow water. I figured Dennis used the pond to water the cattle in the winter.

I got back to the ranch house about three o'clock and was surprised to find Dennis already there. He looked troubled.

"I figured you wouldn't be back till later," I said.

"The wife was slippin' in an' out of consciousness all day." Dennis was worried. "The docs want to try one more procedure, but they don't hold out much hope. I'm afraid I'm goin' to lose her."

I didn't say anything. What can a person say when someone is dying?

"I tried to talk to her, but I don't know if she heard me or comprehended," said Dennis. "What did you do today?"

"Just rode around the hay fields. Everythin' seems well organized."

"You can thank the wife for that," said Dennis. "She saw I was havin' a hard time irrigatin' an' had the hay fields surveyed an' leveled. It sure made it easier. I ain't much of an irrigator, but now I just turn the water out an' it goes where it's supposed to.

"I'll fix supper an' we'll eat early tonight."

"Whatever you say," I said. "I rode the horse called Sparkle today an' he's just as good as Bay Boy."

"The wife says all three are about the same," said Dennis.

I thought I ought to stick around close to Dennis during his troubled times, but didn't know what to say. Every time I said something, Dennis had an answer that referred to his wife. They'd been together a long time building up this ranch and Dennis gave all the credit to his wife.

"Tomorrow," said Dennis, "We'll ride up on top of the mountain. We have to take the long way around, there's too much shale to take what looks like the short way. We'll gather what cattle are on top an' push 'em down lower. It'll make the gather easier. But we'll still have to ride it again."

The next day I saddled the horse called Socks and Dennis saddled the buckskin. We rode out about the same way we'd gone previously.

When we got to the dam on the creek, we saw a rider coming our way.

"It's Jack Thomas," said Dennis. "He's comin' to see me. He ain't got a car an' goes everywhere horseback. We'll wait for him."

When he got close, Dennis hollered, "Hi Jack! What's up?"

Jack waved his hand in acknowledgment but didn't say anything until he got close. He rode his horse up beside Dennis.

"Jack, this is Pete Peterson. Pete, this is Jack Thomas, my neighbor. Pete's helpin' me out on the fall gather."

Jack nodded in my direction and I nodded back.

"Dennis, I got some news for you. The phone rang about three o'clock this morning. Peggy died today."

Jack was direct.

Dennis looked shocked. "I should have stayed at the hospital longer!" He mumbled his words. "The doc said he thought she had a fair chance. I should have put in a phone like the wife said years ago."

"I'm sorry," said Jack.

"Yeah," replied Dennis. "Thanks. We were goin' to ride the ridge so I could show Pete around, but I guess I'll have to go back now."

"I can show your hired man around," said Jack. "You'd best go to town and take care of things."

"Yeah," said Dennis. "Pete, you go with Jack."

"Sure," I said.

Dennis turned his horse around and started back to the ranch without another word.

Jack said, "I feel sorry for him. I had to bring the news to him and Peg when their son died. They don't have a phone."

"They had a son?" I questioned.

"Yes. He didn't have much interest in running the ranch. Went to college to be a lawyer. Dennis didn't like that, he wanted the boy to continue in his footsteps. But Peg insisted and argued that Dennis Junior would be happier and do better as a lawyer. He had a law degree but was killed in a car wreck soon after he graduated and passed the bar exam."

"I didn't know that," I said.

"Dennis doesn't talk about him much, but I think he was secretly very proud of him."

"No other kids?" I asked.

"No."

We started our horses toward the ridge without speaking.

I was curious about Jack. He was an Indian, but didn't speak broken English or with an accent like many Indians. As far as I could tell, he spoke perfect English.

The climb up to the top of the ridge was tough. It was a narrow and steep trail we followed, bordered on both sides by lodgepole pine trees. It was a steep dropoff on the downhill side. Our horses were breathing hard by the time we got to the top even though we'd stopped frequently to rest them.

I thought there wouldn't be many cattle up this high, especially if they didn't have water.

When we reached the top, we gave our horses a long rest. There was a lot of grass on the top of the ridge and there were clumps of lodgepole pines scattered around. I could see some cattle in the distance.

"Where do the cattle get water?" I asked.

"There's a spring farther south," answered Jack. "It runs year round and it's good cold water. We'll ride over to it. The trail we came up on leads to it. We'll ride over to it and water the horses."

I took in the view. From here, I could see mountain ranges off to the east and west and the whole valley below me. It was quite a sight and I wished I had a camera. But I didn't.

We followed the trail toward the spring. We passed a strange assortment of rocks that looked out of place against the low rock-covered hill.

"What's that?" I asked.

Jack looked surprised. "You noticed that?"

"Yeah," I said. "It looks very much out of place where it is."

"That is a hastily made fort."

"It don't look like a fort to me," I said.

"Years ago there was a battle between the Utes and Shoshone Indians here. The Utes were up here cutting poles for their tepees and were surprised by the Shoshones that came up here to cut poles. A fight between them followed and the

Utes hastily gathered up what rocks, brush, and trees that they could and built that as a defense. The Shoshone eventually defeated the Utes and took the poles they'd cut as their own. I've found a lot of arrowheads around there."

I asked, "How do you know this story?"

"My grandfather's father was in the battle. He got an arrow in the leg and walked with a limp the rest of his life. He had the arrowhead in his leg when he died. Even with the arrowhead in his leg, he lived a long time, although I never talked to him. He died before I was born. The story has been passed down through each generation to me."

"Interestin'," I said. "You probably know a lot of the history of this country."

"Yes," replied Jack, without volunteering any more information.

I thought if I was going to get any more information about the early days of the country, I was going to have to pry it out of him.

"All the Utes were killed?" I asked.

"Yes," replied Jack. "It was a bloody battle with a lot of dead and wounded on each side."

We rode on to the spring. We passed a lot of cattle on the way and I was surprised at how many cattle there were up here.

At the spring, we watered the horses.

"We'll go farther and bring all the cattle. We'll push them down to the river and they'll be easier to gather. Dennis does this every year. One year, he missed a cow and she got snowed in up here. She was wild and about half crazy the following spring when we found her."

"I'd bet it would be tough goin' comin' up here in the winter," I said.

"Yes," said Jack. "The snow drifts into that canyon we came up and it'll be fifteen or twenty feet deep. That's the only way up here."

We rode on farther until we came to the end of the ridge. From here we could see the whole valley.

Jack pointed to the bottom of the valley. "That's Dennis's place down there."

From up here, I got a good look at the ranch. I could see the whole place and it looked very similar to what I'd imagined it would look like from the air.

"Where's your place," I asked.

"It's over there," replied Jack. "You can't see it from here because of the mountain. It's actually closer to Dennis's coming by the river than taking the road."

"Dennis told me you don't have a car."

"That's correct," said Jack.

"How come?"

"Don't need one. Dennis will take me to town occasionally for groceries, or he and Peg will bring me some supplies."

"That's kinda tough livin' ain't it?" I asked.

"Not really," answered Jack. "In some respects, the old ways are better than the modern ways. But I do have electricity and a phone at my place. I like that. I just don't need a car, I can get anywhere I want to go horseback. And I have some good horses.

"We'd better split up and start gathering cattle. You head off to the west, I'll go to the east and we'll meet at the spring then push them down."

Jack left without another word and I made a circle around to the west. I gathered close to a hundred head of cows and calves and met Jack at the spring. He'd gotten about as many cows as I did and we started them back down the ridge without a word.

It was slow going down the canyon and Jack got in the middle of the herd to keep the herd moving. The cattle had to go single file down the trail and it was slow going. In a few places, I had to get off the trail to turn back a cow that had wandered off and I was grateful that Socks was sure footed. Some of the banks we had to go down were steep and in a place or two, Socks had a tough time getting back up to the trail. But he made it.

When I made it to the mouth of the canyon, Jack was waiting.

"We'll push them to the dam and turn them loose," said Jack. "Some of them will work their way back up the canyons, but not many will get to the top of the ridge."

We got to the dam and let the cattle go. We watered the horses then Jack said, "I've got to go home," and left without another word.

I said, "So long," and Jack just waved his hand.

As I rode back to the ranch, I thought, *I'd sure like to pick his brain about the history of this country. I bet I could learn a lot.*

I got to the ranch, gave Socks a good rub down, fed the horses from the pickup and went to the house to fix my own supper.

I found everything I needed. The dishes were still in the dishwasher, but they had been cleaned. I put them away, keeping out what I needed.

Supper was pretty plain that night. It consisted of warmed-up leftovers. I watched the local news on television that night and was a little surprised to see that Margret Jorgenson's passing away was an item. Apparently, the Jorgenson's were well known in the area. The news didn't mention anything about a funeral, but there would be a memorial service held in two days.

I was surprised to find Dennis at the ranch the next morning, fixing breakfast.

After the initial hellos, I asked, "You all right? I never heard you come in last night."

"Yep," replied Dennis. "There ain't nothin' I can do in town, so I came home. What'd you do yesterday?"

"I rode with Jack an' we pushed a lot of cattle off the ridge. We let 'em go at the dam."

"Good," said Dennis.

"I put the dishes from last night in the dishwasher but didn't turn it on. I don't know how to operate it. I saw on the TV that your wife's memorial service is tomorrow. You're not havin' a funeral?"

"Nope. She wanted to be cremated an' have her ashes scattered up on the ridge. I'll take her up when we go up next time. You want to go to the memorial?"

I didn't really want to go, but out of consideration for Dennis, I said, "Yes."

"I'll pick up Jack in the mornin' an' we'll go."

"I don't have a suit," I said.

"I ain't either," said Dennis. "Really don't need one an' Peg wouldn't know me in one."

"We ain't got much to do today. I want to water the hay one more time before the snow starts. Give it a good waterin' now an' the hay will come good in the spring an' it'll provide a little more feed for the cattle. You can ride out with me if you want, but there won't be anythin' for you to do."

"I'll go," I said, thinkin' my company might be good for Dennis.

We saddled up, Dennis got a shovel and we rode out. I was glad Dennis didn't get a shovel for me! I followed Dennis out to the dam. I opened all the gates horseback as Dennis was carrying a shovel. Along the way, Dennis used the shovel to clean out some tumbleweeds that had blown into the ditch without getting off his horse. At the dam, Dennis opened the gate and started the water toward the hay fields. We rode back, following the water. On the hay fields, we rode along the main ditch and Dennis cleaned out more tumbleweeds.

On the main ditch, Dennis had installed head gates. He made sure they were all opened. When we got to the end of the ditch and all the head gates were open, Dennis said, "We're done with that now. We can call it a day."

"Aren't you goin' to check the water?" I asked.

"Nope. It'll take care of itself. It'll take three days to cover the ground, then I'll go shut it off. The excess water will fill up that catch pond at the bottom of the fields."

"Most outfits keep a close eye on the water," I said.

"I don't have to. I used to, but the wife convinced me to put in the head gates in such a manner that each head gate becomes a spillway dam. I don't think she liked me wakin' up in the middle of the night to change the water. The water runs onto the field, but the main part of the stream continues down the ditch to the next little dam.

"I'm really glad she convinced me to do it. I didn't much care for gettin' up at night to change the water. Course, I'd check it every few hours when we first put it in, but it worked an' I quit checkin' it. Sure made my irrigatin' easier!"

We rode back to the barn along the ditch. I saw how the water backed up behind the spillway dams, yet continued to go down the ditch.

CHAPTER 9

At the barn, Dennis said, "We're done for today. You just take it easy this afternoon. Supper will be ready at six."

I was about to ask if he wanted any company, but kept quiet. I didn't know what I could say that would take his mind off his wife's passing.

The next morning, I fed the horses before breakfast. At breakfast, I told Dennis, "I've already fed the horses. I'll grab a shower, put on some clean clothes an' be ready to go to the memorial right directly."

"I need a shower too," said Dennis. "You come to the house when you're ready an' we'll go to town when I'm ready."

I showered in the bunkhouse, put on a clean white shirt, clean pants and was ready. I met Dennis in the living room. He was watching the news on television and they were announcing the memorial service for Margret Jorgenson.

When the broadcast was over, Dennis said, "It's time to go. We better leave now, we have to pick up Jack, an' it's a long ways around to his place."

When we left the house, Dennis locked the house, went to the barn and locked it. "I don't normally do this, but with all the news about the wife's memorial, I don't want uninvited visitors." We drove to the main gate and Dennis got out, closed the gate and locked it.

"That should keep everyone out," he said, as he got back in the car.

We drove toward town, then turned off the main highway to Jack's place. It took us about an hour to get to Jack's house and when we got there, we found Jack dressed in a suit and tie, ready to go. He made an impressive sight, dressed up as he was.

I was impressed with Jack's house. It was a ranch style brick home. I'd envisioned him living in a tepee or a mud hogan, not having a car and trying to hold onto some of the old ways.

I got in the back seat of the car, letting Jack and Dennis talk in the front seat.

I heard Dennis say, "We're goin' to church for the memorial. It's been a long time since I been in church, I hope they let me in!"

Even in his mourning, Dennis tried to maintain his sense of humor.

"They'll let you in," said Jack. "They welcome heathens! They think they have a chance to convert them!"

Both men laughed and I enjoyed the humor.

We arrived at the church only to find the parking lot crowded.

"They told me they'd reserve a parkin' space for me," said Dennis.

"There it is," said Jack. "They've got a sign on it, 'RESERVED FOR DENNIS JORGENSEN'. Maybe they don't know you're a heathen!"

Again, both men laughed and the three of us entered the church after Dennis parked the car in the reserved spot.

I was surprised at the number of people at the church. Apparently the Jorgensen's were well thought of in the area. I recognized Charlie and Bob from the ranch where I'd halter broke the mustangs. I also saw George Cooper and Davy Jones from Howard Wells' outfit.

Dennis and Jack knew everybody and after they'd visited with Charlie and Bob, I had a chance to visit with them. They seemed pleased to see me as I shook hands with them.

"I'm ridin' some horses you trained," I told

Charlie. "An' they're just as good as everythin' else I rode on your outfit."

"I'm glad to hear that," said Charlie. "I do remember sellin' some bay horses to Peg. I hadn't heard where you landed, but if you got on with Dennis, you got on with a good man."

"I got on with Dennis," I said.

"Looks like you'll be fillin' in for Peg. She was a good hand, better than most men. But I'm sure you'll do a good job."

Charlie, Bob and I visited a little longer then I went to George Cooper.

"I heard that Howard had died," I said. "Sorry." I really wasn't sorry, I could have cared less, but felt I had to say it.

"Yeah," said George. "It wasn't the wreck that killed him, it was all that booze. I told him more than once it would kill him, but he wouldn't listen. He had the habit bad."

"How are things out on the place now?" I asked.

"The family has made me manager. Maybe I can make it a goin' concern now," said George.

"Good luck," I said. "The service is about to start. I'd better get a seat."

I sat down beside Dennis. Jack was on the other side of him.

Dennis introduced me to everyone that came by before the service began, but I doubted if I'd remember them all.

The service started with the preacher telling of Margret's life. When he said "Margret had donated a lot of money to the church, even though she didn't attend regularly," I heard Dennis whisper to Jack, "So that's where all my money went!"

Jack smiled and grunted.

There were a lot of nice things said about Missus Jorgensen, mostly about how good of a hand she was on the ranch and what a help she'd been to Dennis.

Again, Dennis whispered to Jack, "Help! If the truth were known, she was my boss!"

Jack again smiled and grunted.

I couldn't tell if Dennis's comments were truthful or if he was trying to make the situation easier on himself.

When the memorial was over and we were leaving, so many good things had been said about what a nice person Missus Jorgensen had been and what a good horse woman she was, that I found myself wishing I'd have known her.

Dennis got the ashes of his wife and the three of us went to the car. We were the last ones to leave as there were a lot of people saying good-bye to Dennis and expressing their condolences. I saw Charlie again and said goodbye.

Charlie asked, "Have you made any plans for next year? I saw Claude here today an' he asked if I wanted more mustang yearlings to halter break. He was impressed with the job you'd done."

I told Charlie, "My only plans at this time are to help Dennis through the fall gather. Then I don't know what I'll do."

"You keep in touch," said Charlie.

The drive back to Jack's seemed long. I sat in the back seat and Dennis and Jack sat in the front. They made plans for the gather and set a date to start.

Dennis told Jack, "We need to get 'em in before the snow flies, especially off the ridge. It don't take long for that draw to fill up with snow."

Jack agreed and I heard Jack say, "I saw one of my cows with yours when Pete and I pushed them off the ridge."

"We'll just take her to my place an' I'll bring her over to your place after we've weaned," said Dennis.

"Don't forget to bring her calf!" said Jack.

Both men laughed and I was sure Dennis wouldn't try to steal the calf.

We dropped Jack off at his ranch and I got into the front seat of the car. The ride to Dennis's ranch was quiet. I didn't have anything to say and Dennis was quiet. I thought he was reflecting on the memorial service.

At the ranch, Dennis took the ashes inside and said, "Breakfast at six."

I went to the bunkhouse without saying anything and went to bed. I was tired even though I hadn't done anything all day.

The next morning Dennis said, "We'll ride down to the pond an' see how it's fillin' up. If it's pretty full, I can open up a gate an' let some out. I don't want it washin' out the dam."

We saddled up. I saddled Bay Boy and Dennis saddled up the paint. He didn't take a shovel.

The pond was about half full when we got to it.

"Two more days of lettin' the water run, an' the pond will be full," said Dennis. "The whole place will be irrigated an' I won't have to worry about it till spring."

We rode back to the barn and turned the horses loose.

"I've got a bull pasture along the road comin' into the ranch," said Dennis. "Tomorrow we'll ride fence an' make sure the bulls will stay home. It'll probably take us all day. Supper is at six."

I went to the bunkhouse thinking, *So far this job ain't had a lot for me to do! I'll be glad when we start the gather, it'll mean more ridin'. I think Dennis might be dreamin' up jobs just to keep me around until the gather starts!*

The next morning, I saddled Socks and Dennis saddled his black. He handed me a canvas bag full of fence staples and a hammer. I hung it on my saddle. He hung a bag filled with the same on his saddle. I noticed he didn't include a fence stretcher.

"I don't expect they'll be much to do until we get to the far side on the east. The snow drifts into a little draw over there an' there's always a lot of fence fixin' there. If it's too bad, we'll come out in the truck an' fix it proper."

I just nodded. I didn't think much of fence fixing, but it was part of the job and came with the territory.

When we got to the gate into the bull pasture, Dennis said, "You head off to the right an' I'll go left. We'll meet on the other side. That's where I expect the fence will need the most repair."

We parted and I rode fence, knocking in some staples that had worked loose due to the freezing and thawing of the previous year. I didn't have to get off Socks to do it.

At one point, I came across a deer carcass hung up in the fence. The deer had tried to jump the fence and got a hind leg caught between the two top wires. Caught as he was, he starved to death.

Socks was a little reluctant to approach the carcass so I got off him, hobbled him and went to cut the carcass from the fence. Most horses don't like to approach dead animals, the smell warns them that something has died.

I freed the carcass from the fence, then got the hammer and using it like a winch, tightened both top wires.

I got back on Socks and continued on. I used the hammer to knock in loose staples until I got to the draw. Again, I didn't need to get off Socks to do it.

When I got into the draw, the fence was in good shape, better than I expected from what Dennis had told me. I was pleased and thought this job would be easier than I'd imagined. However, it wasn't long before I changed my mind. I'd come to a stretch of fence that was completely down.

I looked over the situation, got off Socks, hobbled him, got the bag of staples and hammer and started fixing fence. A few of the posts were laying over and I tried to straighten them.

I got the posts fairly straight and started to fasten the wire to them. I was making a suspension fence. The wire was holding the fence posts up. I was busy and didn't see Dennis come riding up.

"Got a pretty bad stretch here," he said.

The sound of his voice surprised me for a second. I was bent over pounding in a staple on the bottom wire.

I straightened up and said, "Yeah."

"Well," said Dennis, "don't worry about it."

For a split second, I thought we were going to abandon the fence fixing and was pleased.

But Dennis continued, "There's another bad stretch where I came from. I didn't even try to fix it, just rode by. I think we'll have to go back and get the truck, more posts an' wire an' come back an' fix it right tomorrow. Just leave the fence as it is. You can leave the hammer an' staples hangin' on a post here."

I did as I was told and caught Socks. He'd been grazing not too far from where I'd left him. I got on and Dennis and I started back to the ranch.

The wind had started and it was noticeably colder.

"Winter's on its way," said Dennis.

"I thought I'd noticed somethin' different," I said. "Think I'll get my shotgun chaps out."

I'd been wearing chink chaps, a shorter, summer chap.

"You won't need chaps tomorrow," said Dennis. "We'll be afoot all day."

"From the feel of that wind, I'll need 'em, just for warmth," I said. "I'd rather be too warm than too cold."

"You might be right."

We got to the ranch, unsaddled the horses and fed them.

"Supper's at six," said Dennis. "You just relax till then."

I went to the bunkhouse and relaxed. I thought, *There's been a lot of relaxin' time on this job.*

Just before six, I walked to the house. The wind had gotten colder and stronger.

"The winter's sure enough comin'," said Dennis.

"Yep," I said. "I've noticed the horses have been sheddin' their summer coats an' growin' their winter coats. You know they shed twice a year an' while they're sheddin', they're growin' the new coat."

"I know that," said Dennis. "I been watchin'. Tomorrow, we'll feed an' go fix fence. Better bring your winter coat. I figure we got at least two more days of fence fixin'."

After supper, I went to the bunkhouse. I got my winter coat out of the car on the way. The coat would be warmer in the bunkhouse than in the car overnight. I was not looking forward to fixing fence, but it had to be done.

The next day, we fixed fence. We dug a couple of postholes, planted a post in each one and stretched new wire.

"If we put a couple of stays between each post, it might help keep the fence up," I said. "They got wire stays in the hardware store in town, but wooden stays have been the old way."

"That's a good idea, but I ain't goin' to town just to get stays," said Dennis. "We can go on the forest an' get a bunch."

We got the part of the fence fixed that I'd been working on the day before and moved on to the part that Dennis had passed over.

We both sat in the truck, a little reluctant to get out. I looked over the situation and decided we'd have to come back tomorrow before the fence was completely repaired.

"Well," I said, getting out of the truck, "the sooner we get started, the sooner we'll be done."

Dennis got out of the truck. "You got that right!"

I could tell he didn't like fixing fence any more than I did.

We worked on the fence until around four o'clock then went back to the ranch.

We ate supper silently and Dennis finally said, "You don't much like fixin' fence, do you?"

"Nope," I replied.

"Well, I don't either! But it has to be done. The Missus didn't mind it so much, she always said fixin' fence was easier than goin' out lookin' for missin' cattle. I guess she was right, but I'd rather be ridin'."

"Me too," I replied.

"We should finish up this fence fixin' tomorrow. The next day, we'll go up on the forest an' cut some stays. The next day, we'll put 'em up then we'll be done, at least till next year."

"Good," I said.

It was cold the next day and I was glad I'd put on my shotgun chaps. There was some rain and I thought I'd seen some snowflakes in the rain.

Dennis also noticed the snowflakes in the rain and said, "There'll be snow up on the ridge."

We finished with the fence two days later after going to the forest to get stays. Dennis took a chainsaw and cut small trees for stays and I cut off the limbs with an axe and loaded them into the truck.

CHAPTER 10

It continued to rain. The morning after we finished the fence, Dennis said, "I think I'll go over to Jack's an' tell him we're goin' to start the gather tomorrow. It's a little early, but it's been snowin' up on the ridge. I don't want them cattle to get snowed in. You want to go to Jack's with me? There ain't nothin' to do here today."

"Might just as well," I said.

We left the ranch and Dennis closed and locked the gate.

"I keep this gate locked when I ain't around. It keeps the strangers off an' it lets friends know I ain't here."

We went to Jack's. I don't know why, but I liked the man. He didn't talk much and I knew if a feller was going to get any information out of him, he'd have to pry it.

Upon arriving at Jack's, he invited us in.

"Coffee's on the stove," he said. "Help yourself."

Dennis got a cup. "Wanna cup?" he asked me.

"Nope," I replied. "I'm full of coffee."

I looked around Jack's living room and kitchen. There were a lot of Indian ornaments decorating the living room and I wanted to question Jack about them, but Jack and Dennis were making plans to gather cattle.

Jack's kitchen had all the modern appliances from a coffee maker to a dishwasher. There was a television in the living room. I wondered about the man. He had all the modern conveniences, yet didn't have a car. He went everywhere horseback. He seemed to mix the modern ways with the old ways. I wanted to question him about it, but didn't. He was able to choose his own lifestyle.

I turned my attention to the conversation between Jack and Dennis.

Dennis was saying, "I want to get all my cows off the ridge before the snow gets too deep. It's snowed up there the last couple of days an' it might be pretty deep where it's drifted into the canyon."

Jack simply agreed without saying anything.

"I want to start in the morning," Dennis continued. "Do you want to come an' help us?"

"You know I do," said Jack. "I'll be there at the regular time."

"Good," said Dennis. "It's a little early, but there's plenty of feed on the hay fields."

The men continued to visit and rehash old times. I was content to listen.

Soon Dennis said, "Well, we've got to hurry back to do nothin'."

"No need to rush off," said Jack. "I don't get much company here as it is."

"We better get goin'," said Dennis. "It's getting late."

I looked at my watch. It was mid-afternoon. Listening to Jack and Dennis talk had been interesting and the time flew by.

On the way back to the ranch, I said, "Jack's living room appears to be very much like a museum. He's got a lot of interestin' stuff in there."

"Yeah. He's tryin' to preserve the old ways, at least part of 'em. He can tell you a story about everything in there."

"I'd like to hear it," I said.

"Jack tells me he's goin' to donate it all to the Indian museum the other side of town when he dies. I told him he'd better do it before he dies because after he's dead, he can't do nothin'!"

We both laughed at Dennis's comment and rode to the ranch in silence.

After supper, Dennis said, "You better dress warm tomorrow. It'll be cold up there on that ridge, especially if the winds blowin'."

The next morning we saddled up and headed to the ridge. Dennis had hung a canvas bag on his saddle.

"What's that?" I asked.

"That's the Missus's ashes. I'm goin' to scatter 'em on the ridge just as she wanted."

I didn't say anything.

When we got to the dam, Dennis shut the water off to the hay fields. Jack was waiting for us.

"Mornin', Jack!"

Jack nodded and I nodded back.

"I plumb forgot about the water, we was havin' so much fun fixin' fence," said Dennis. "The Missus used to remind me about such things. I'm tendin' to get a little forgetful in my old age."

"You ain't that old, are you?" I asked.

"Today, I'm as old as I ever been!" We both laughed at his comment.

"From what I know of your younger days, you're lucky to have made it this long!" said Jack.

Dennis laughed. "You might be right!"

Jack looked at the canvas bag on Dennis's saddle. "That Peg?"

"Yeah," answered Dennis.

"You're lucky she took a liking to you," said Jack. "If she hadn't, you'd have been either in jail or dead a long time ago."

"You're right again," said Dennis. "When are you goin' to be wrong so I can correct you?"

Both men laughed and I thought it was some sort of inside joke. I didn't ask any questions.

We started toward the canyon that led to the top of the ridge. Snow had accumulated on the trail, and it was snowing lightly.

When we got to the canyon, we started up in single file. Dennis led, Jack followed, and I brought up the rear. It was getting colder, but I was glad we were horseback and not fixing fence or some other ranch chore that could only be done on foot.

"We shouldn't get snowed in today," said Dennis.

"No," replied Jack. "But we could have if we'd started later in the week. Look how it's starting to drift already."

I'd noticed that in some areas the snow was about a foot to eighteen inches deep. I didn't realize it had snowed that much.

"There's some cows comin' down the trail," said Dennis. "They'll have to turn around, we ain't got room to let 'em pass. There's a wide spot up ahead, we can get around 'em there."

The cows didn't want to turn around and they went down a pretty steep embankment to get out of our way. One of the cows slipped and fell. She rolled over but got back on her feet.

"That cow all right?" asked Dennis. "I can't see her from here."

"She's okay," I said as I watched the cow regain her balance. "Just got a slight limp."

We continued on. When we topped out on the ridge, it was snowing hard and the wind was blowing.

"Pete, what direction did you go last time you were up here?" asked Dennis.

"I went to the west," I answered.

"You go that way again. You're already familiar with that area. Jack, you go east. I'll go to the far end. Push everything to the center of the meadow. Pete, don't let anythin' start down any of the tops of the canyons. I'm thinkin' the cows won't want to stay up here in the snow, an' we might have a pretty easy day, other than it bein' cold. We'll meet at the pond."

I headed off to the west. I found a few cows

and started them back to the east. Farther along, I found three cows and their calves starting to head down one of the canyons. As fast as I dared go on the snow, I got around them and started them back up to the top of the ridge. They didn't want to go back up on top and I had a hard time pushing them back up. It took longer than I wanted.

When I finally got them on top, I met Dennis coming toward me.

"You okay?" he asked.

I didn't answer immediately, but started the cows toward the cattle in the middle of the meadow. When I had them trotting toward the other cattle, I let them go and answered Dennis.

"I'm okay," I said. "I just had a hard time convincin' them cows that was the wrong way down."

"I come lookin' for you thinkin' you might have fallen off your horse or somethin'," said Dennis.

"Me? Fall off Bay Boy? I like this horse too much to let him go! But we did have to go slow. It's pretty steep down there an' it's slick. I thought he was goin' to slide an' go down a couple of times."

"Looks like you both survived," said Dennis.

"Jack's with the other cattle waitin' for us in the meadow."

"Did I take that long gatherin' them three cows an' calves?" I asked.

"Yep," replied Dennis. "I rode what you didn't cover. Didn't find no cattle an' when I met Jack, I come lookin' for you. I'm sure glad you got them three. You did a good job. Other hands, like them two drifters you replaced, would have let 'em go an' said there weren't any cattle over there."

I grinned at Dennis. "Are you tellin' me I replaced two men? That means double wages!"

Dennis looked a little shocked until he saw that I was smiling. When he realized I was just joking, he said, "I'd sure pay double wages if you could be in two different spots at the same time! If you could have done that, I'd have stayed home by the heater!"

I laughed.

As we rode toward where Jack was holding the cattle he'd found, I asked Dennis, "Did you scatter your wife's ashes? I see the bag still hangin' on your saddle."

"Yep," answered Dennis. "I scattered her ashes at the end of the ridge where she liked to look down on the ranch. She might be able to keep an eye on me there."

I hadn't noticed but I'd worked up a sweat getting the three cows and was starting to feel chilled. I'd be glad to get to the bunkhouse.

We rode toward Jack in silence. The three of us had only gathered around twenty cows and calves. When Jack saw us coming, he started the cattle toward the canyon we'd come up. We got to the head of the canyon and Jack got in the middle of the small bunch of cattle we'd gathered just to keep them moving. It really helped where the cattle had to go single file.

We got to the dam and turned the cattle loose.

"Tomorrow," said Dennis, "we'll put all the cattle we gather in the holdin' pasture. We'll start with the canyon next to the one we just rode an' work our way back, checkin' each canyon. We'll have to ride each canyon probably at least twice to get all the cattle. You comin' tomorrow, Jack?"

"Yes," replied Jack. "I'll be here at the same time. So long."

Jack turned his horse and headed toward his ranch. He didn't say what time he'd be here and I figured both men had done this enough in the past that they knew how long it would take them to get to the dam.

Dennis and I rode back to the ranch without

talking much. At one point, Dennis said, "There's something final about death, ain't there?"

I simply answered "Yep," and thought Dennis was reflecting about his wife's passing. I thought it best to leave him alone with his thoughts.

"Supper will be a little late tonight," said Dennis. "Come to the house an' warm up while I'm fixin' it."

It had been getting colder all afternoon and when we got to the ranch, after tending to the horses, I built a fire in the stove in the bunkhouse. The bunkhouse would be warm after supper.

At supper, Dennis said, "It's goin' to snow tonight. They'll be a couple of inches of snow on the ground in the mornin', you mark my words!"

"I wouldn't doubt that at all," I said. "It'll probably be colder as well!"

Dennis said, "I'll put somethin' in the Crockpot in the mornin' an' it'll be ready when we get back tomorrow night."

After supper, I got my cowboy boot overshoes out of the truck. If I could keep my feet from getting wet, they'd be warmer.

I put some more wood in the stove in the bunkhouse, hoping I wouldn't have to get up in the middle of the night and rebuild the fire. My hopes weren't met. I had to get up around two o'clock and keep the fire going.

At breakfast Dennis asked, "You get cold last night?"

"Yep. I had to get up an' stoke the fire."

"I should of thought," said Dennis. "I got a space heater I don't use. When we're done eatin' I'll give it to you. Plug it in before we leave an' the bunkhouse will be warm when we get back."

"I'll do that, an' I appreciate it!"

The next morning, I saddled Socks and Dennis saddled his paint. I plugged in the space heater before we left. We rode to the dam, leaving the gate to the hay field open behind us, and met Jack, waiting for us. He was wearing a heavier coat.

"Been waitin' long?" asked Dennis.

"About ten minutes," replied Jack. "It's a little colder this morning."

"It's colder than a mother-in-law's kiss, as I suspect Pete would say," said Dennis.

"I wouldn't say that if there were any mothers-in-law around," I said.

"There ain't no mothers-in-law around, so you can say anything you want," said Dennis. "Let's get goin', it ain't goin' to get any warmer real soon."

We rode toward the far canyons. When we got to the next to last canyon before the canyon we'd rode yesterday, Dennis said, "Jack, you ride this canyon an' Pete an' me will ride the next one. We'll meet here in the bottom."

Jack headed up the canyon without saying anything and Dennis headed for the next canyon. We'd passed a lot of cattle in the bottom, heading to the canyons.

In the canyon, Dennis said, "You ride the right side, I'll ride the left. Push everythin' to the middle an' we'll start 'em down."

I didn't say anything and started up the right side of the canyon. The cattle I found, I pushed to the middle of the canyon. I didn't find many, but saw a lot of deer.

I got to the head of the canyon, saw that I couldn't go up any farther because of the shale, found a few more cattle and started following them down the canyon. I swung around to the left and met Dennis pushing cows to the middle. The canyon was wide and there weren't any steep, narrow trails I had to follow, but it was tough going on Socks. The new snow made the footing slick and I thought he was going to go down a couple of times.

When I met Dennis, he asked, "Have any trouble?"

"Nope," I replied. "You?"

"Ol' Paint here went down once," answered Dennis. "Slipped on the snow, but he's all right."

I noticed a big wet spot on the paint's right hip and there was some hair missing.

"We'll go meet Jack."

We'd been gone a few hours and it was early afternoon.

We met Jack. He'd found some cattle and started them down toward the dam.

"I saw your cow in the bunch, Jack," said Dennis. "We'll take her to the ranch. I didn't see her calf."

Jack just nodded.

When we got to the dam, Dennis said, "We can handle 'em from here. The gates are all open to the hay fields."

"Then I'll go home," said Jack. "Don't lose my cow!" Both men laughed.

"There's little chance of loosin' her on the hay fields," said Dennis.

Jack started to head out. Before he left, he said, "Same time tomorrow?"

"Yep," replied Dennis.

Dennis and I followed the cattle to the holding pasture. We left the gate into the holding pasture open. Dennis went ahead and opened the gate on the entrance coming from the ranch. He counted the cattle as they went through the gate. I pushed the cattle through the gate slowly, so Dennis could get a good count.

When the last of the cattle passed through the gate, Dennis hollered, "Close the gate! I'll go ahead an' make sure the cattle don't miss the hay field. Don't leave any cows in the tall brush!"

I waved at Dennis to let him know I'd heard him and he started off at a fast trot.

I followed the cattle. It was back and forth through the brush, making sure no cows were hiding out. It was slow going. I figured I was riding two hundred yards for every one hundred yards the cattle went toward the hay field. But that was herding cattle.

There was a lot of snow on the tall brush and a lot of it came off on me as I rode through the brush. My chaps and coat were getting wet and I was glad I'd plugged in the space heater before we left. The warm bunkhouse would help dry off the chaps and coat.

I thought to myself, *I'd better get up early an' oil*

my chaps in the mornin' when they're dry. It'll help wa-
terproofin' 'em.

Dennis was waiting for me as I pushed the last of the cattle through the gate onto the hay field. He closed the gate.

Surveying me, he said, "Got a little wet comin' through the brush, huh?"

"Yep," I answered. "I didn't get this wet just spittin'!"

Dennis laughed and said, "I got some waterproofin' at the house. You're welcome to it, if you want."

"I got some in the car," I said.

"The stuff I got, you can put it on while the leather's wet. Soaks in better."

"I'll give it a try, if you don't mind," I said.

While Dennis fixed supper, I oiled my chaps.

The next few days were spent gathering the canyons then reriding the canyons we'd gathered previously. Jack came each day riding a different horse.

One day, Jack said, "I saw my cow in that bunch and her calf."

"We'll sort her off an' I'll bring her over to you in the truck," said Dennis.

"Just don't forget her calf!" said Jack. Both men laughed.

Dennis counted each bunch of cattle as we put them through the gate into the hay field.

On the last day, Dennis said, "That about does it. Accordin' to my figures, there's eight hundred thirty-nine cows. I'm short one cow. You got her over to your place, Jack?"

Jack laughed. "I don't think so, but I haven't looked at my cows for a few days. She could be there."

"Maybe I ought to keep your cow till you return mine!" said Dennis.

There was some good natured bickering going on between the two men and I was sure they knew each other well enough to joke about something as serious as stealing a cow.

"You goin' to start your gather tomorrow, Jack?"

"Yes."

"Well," replied Dennis, "Pete an' I will be over to help. Same time?"

"Yes."

CHAPTER 11

Jack left and returned to his ranch. Dennis and I rode back to the ranch, took care of the horses, and had supper.

After supper, Dennis said, "Tomorrow we'll help Jack. We'll need to start earlier. Breakfast at five."

"I'll be there," I said.

When we finished breakfast, Dennis put stuff for supper in the Crockpot.

"It'll be late when we get back," said Dennis. "But supper will be ready."

I saddled Sparkle, Dennis saddled his black and we rode toward Jack's. At the dam, we went in the direction Jack always went toward his place. This was new country to me and I looked it all over carefully as we rode.

"Lookin' for cows, Pete?"

"Not really. This is new country an' I want to keep my bearin's," I replied.

"No need to look for cattle," said Dennis. "Jack would have pushed 'em all down when he went back. Our gather will start over on his west side. This will be our toughest day here. We won't get back to my place till well after dark."

"I still need to keep my bearin's," I said.

"Won't do you much good after dark," said Dennis. "If you're worried about getting' lost, ol' Sparkle can always find his way home."

"I ain't worried about gettin' lost," I said. "An' I know my horse can always get home. I just like to know where I am an' where I been. However, where I'm goin' has always been somewhat of a problem!"

Dennis laughed.

About an hour after we left the dam, we met Jack at a gate. After the initial greetings, we went through the gate and rode toward the west.

Soon, we stopped and Jack said, "Dennis, you go off here and push everything to the east and north. Pete and I will gather the west side and meet you at the gate to my property."

Jack was in charge and I figured it was proper. It was his cattle we were gathering. When we gathered Dennis's cattle, Dennis gave the orders.

Dennis left and Jack and I continued to the east.

"This is BLM ground we're on now," said Jack. "My property borders it on the east side."

We rode for a spell then Jack said, "You ride this area. Check the little meadow on the east side when you've started what cattle you've found to the north. Put them all together then push them north until you come to the mouth of a big canyon on the west. Wait for me there. I'll be bringing what cattle I've found down the canyon."

I did as I was told and it wasn't long before I'd gathered about seventy or eighty cows and their calves. I checked the little meadow, found a few more cows and started everything to the southeast. At the mouth of the big canyon, I let the cattle continue and started up the big canyon.

Going up the canyon, I met some cattle that had started down. I let them go and continued up the canyon. Soon I saw Jack, behind a large bunch of cattle. He was having some trouble. The cattle kept spreading out on him and he was having a tough time keeping them headed in the right direction.

I got around the herd and started helping move the cattle in the right direction. That made it easier on Jack.

When I got close to Jack, I could see that

his horse was well lathered up. He'd had a real tough time.

We finally got the cattle into a semblance of a herd and had them headed toward the mouth of the canyon. When we got to the mouth of the canyon, we mixed the cattle Jack had found with the cattle I'd left there and started them to the east.

When the cattle were started east, Jack waved me over. I rode over to him.

"I need to give my horse a rest," he said. "We've had some tough going!"

"I see." I said, noticing again Jack's lathered horse.

"I'm sure glad you came up the canyon to help me," he said. "If you hadn't, I'd have still been up there. But I think I've got all of them. There's a fence about a mile farther and that will make it easier to move them. We'll meet Dennis at the gate. He'll hold everything at the gate and I can count them through."

Jack gave his horse a good rest then we followed the cattle to where Dennis was waiting at the gate, without much trouble. Jack slipped through the herd and opened the gate and Dennis and I started pushing the cattle through, slowly.

Jack got his count and when he got done, we met at the gate.

"Looks like you had some hard ridin'," said Dennis.

"Yes," answered Jack. "It was pretty tough until Pete came along and gave me a hand."

"You got most of your cows?" asked Dennis.

"There's about three-quarters of them," replied Jack. "I'm still out about a hundred and fifty. They'll be over on the west side. We shouldn't have a problem gathering them tomorrow."

"Same time?" asked Dennis.

"Yes."

"Then we'll be here," said Dennis. "See you tomorrow. Let's go Pete. It'll be well after dark when we get home."

I hadn't paid any attention to the time, but it was well into the early evening. Dennis and I turned our horses and started toward the ranch.

"Jack's cows ain't as hard to gather as mine," said Dennis. "My country is a little tougher. But I wouldn't trade it. We grow some real big calves on my range."

"I saw some pretty big calves in your herd," I said.

"Yep," replied Dennis. "They'll weight up

pretty good. They always do. I just hope the prices are high when I sell 'em."

We rode to the ranch without saying much, cared for our horses and ate supper.

"It'll be leftovers tomorrow night," said Dennis. "I made plenty. Breakfast at five."

"Okay," I said and went to the bunkhouse. I was more tired than I realized and slept well.

The next morning after breakfast, I saddled Spot and Dennis saddled the buckskin. We rode to Jack's and met him where we did yesterday. The sun was just coming up.

"We're ready for a pretty easy day today," said Dennis.

"I hope it's easier than yesterday," said Jack. "It should be."

We rode to the west and after about an hour, Jack sent Dennis off to the north.

"You know where to wait for us Dennis," said Jack.

"Yep. I'll be there."

Jack and I rode farther to the west and soon, Jack sent me to the north.

"Push everything you find to the south. You'll come to a fence. Wait for me, I'll meet you there," said Jack.

Jack was taking the larger circle and I thought it was right, as I didn't know the country.

I started finding cows as soon as I left Jack. I started them south and rode the country pretty thoroughly, finding more cattle. I mixed the cattle and had a fair sized herd by the time we came to the fence. I found Jack waiting for me and the few cattle he'd found headed east along the fence.

"I was supposed to wait for *you* here," I said.

"I didn't find many cattle and came here. I saw cattle you'd started and waited for you. You found more cattle than I did. We'll just take them along the fence until we meet Dennis. I'll slip ahead of them and keep them along the fence."

Jack left and I pushed the cattle. Jack kept them headed in the right direction and I just kept the tail end of the herd following. The fence helped.

Soon we came upon Dennis, holding the cattle he'd found by the gate. He hadn't found many. I figured I'd gathered as many cattle as Jack and Dennis had.

Jack slipped ahead of the cattle and opened the gate. Dennis went ahead to slow the cattle down as Jack counted them. I backed off a little as I didn't want to push the herd too fast.

When the last cow was through the gate, Jack closed it. He stayed inside. Dennis and I were on the outside.

"Did you see my cow an' calf?" asked Dennis.

"No," replied Jack.

"I saw her," I said. "An' her calf was with her."

"Okay," said Jack. "That makes my count right. I had one too many."

I asked, "Do we have all your cattle?"

"Yep," answered Jack.

"I'll bring your cow over an' pick up my cow in the truck," said Dennis.

Jack asked, "Are you going to bring her calf? Do we need to meet on common ground or can we make the trade on Indian ground?"

Both men laughed at what I thought was a reference to the trouble between the white man and Indian many years ago. I remained silent, thinking it was a private joke.

"We'll sort my calves off the cows tomorrow," said Dennis. "You goin' to come over an' help?"

"Yes," answered Jack. "I feel like I must look after the welfare of my cow that you've got. And her calf." Both men laughed again.

"Bring a pack horse and your bedroll," said Dennis. "You can stay in the bunkhouse with Pete."

"Who's cooking?" asked Jack.

"I am," replied Dennis.

"What's his cooking like, Pete?"

Not wanting to get on the wrong side of Dennis, after careful consideration, I replied, "Well, it's better than mine."

The men laughed again.

"I think I will miss Peg's cooking. Same time?" asked Jack.

"I already miss her cookin'," said Dennis. "Yep, same time. Will you call the truckers an' see when we can get a truck? I think day after tomorrow will work. I think that's Saturday."

"I'll call and I'll be there," said Jack. "It is Saturday, but the trucks will be there whenever they say."

Dennis and I rode back to his ranch. He outlined his plans.

"We'll sort off the calves from the cows tomorrow then the next day sort the steers from the heifers. I'll pick out a few replacement heifers an' we'll ship the rest. I need to go through the cows an' do some cullin' before I start pickin' out replacements."

We rode the rest of the way to the ranch in silence. At the ranch, we cared for the horses then went to the house to eat the leftovers.

During supper, Dennis said, "I'll have to fix somethin' special tomorrow for Jack. You seemed a little reluctant to answer Jack's question about my cookin'. Why?"

Not wanting to get on the wrong side of Dennis, I replied, "It's a lot better than mine."

"Well then, you can't be much of a cook!" said Dennis, laughing.

"I ain't," I replied and joined in the laughter. Wanting to change the subject, I said, "It wasn't too tough a day today."

"The west side of Jack's is always easier to gather," said Dennis.

We watched the news then I went to the bunkhouse.

"Breakfast at six," said Dennis as I left.

Knowing that Jack was going to spend the night, I thought it might be a good idea to sweep it out and clean it up a little. I did it before I turned in.

The next morning as I walked to the house for breakfast, I saw Jack riding in leading a packhorse. I waited for him at the barn.

"Mornin," I said.

"Good morning," replied Jack. "It's getting colder."

"Yep," I replied, noting the colder air. "Winter's on its way."

Jack unsaddled the packhorse and loosened the cinch on his saddle horse then turned them in with the other horses.

"I'll take my bedroll to the bunkhouse," he said. "I'll meet you at the house."

I went to the house where Dennis was fixing breakfast.

"Jack's here," I said.

"Yep. I saw him through the window."

A few minutes later, Jack entered the house. After the initial greetings, Jack said, "You must think a lot of Pete here. I see you furnished him with a space heater. You always made me get up in the middle of the night to keep the fire going."

"Yep," replied Dennis. "Pete's pretty good help."

"Are you insinuating that I'm not?" questioned Jack. Both men laughed.

"Nope," replied Dennis. "I just wanted him to stick around longer!"

Both men laughed again. I thought they were good friends, joking about each other as they did.

After breakfast, Dennis and I saddled our

horses and the three of us went out to gather the cattle. It was an easy gather on the hay fields and we soon had all the cattle corralled.

Dennis had a good set of corrals to work. There was an alley way leading from the big pen where we'd corralled all the cattle and there were plenty of pens on each side of the alley to separate what needed to be separated.

"Pete," said Dennis, "you work this gate for all the calves. Jack, you work this gate for the bulls, your cow an' calf an' what cows I might want to cull. I'll bring 'em to you an' holler where I want them to go. We'll let all the cows into that big pen at the end of the alley way."

Jack and I turned our horses loose in a pen we weren't going to use after loosening the cinches, and manned the gates to the pens. Our work would be on foot the rest of the day.

"Workin' them gates ain't much fun," said Dennis, "but it has to be done. There's some stock whips propped up alongside the alley. Better get 'em, you might need 'em. Some of them bulls are kinda ignorant, don't let 'em get you."

Dennis started bringing cattle down the alley. He was pretty good at separating the calves from the cows, but occasionally Jack and I would have to do some separating on foot.

At one point, Dennis hollered, "Here comes your cow, Jack! Don't let her by you!"

Jack turned the cow into his pen. "Where's her calf?"

"I ain't seen her calf yet," replied Dennis.

"Keep your eyes open for my calf," said Jack. "It's probably the biggest one there."

"No, it'll probably be the smallest one. That'll be pretty tough," said Dennis. "They're all pretty big. The little ones are liable to slip by me."

I laughed at the men. They seemed to be bragging, but it was all in fun.

After a time, Dennis hollered at me, "Move down to the next pen, Pete. Your pen is gettin' pretty full. You'll have an easier time of it."

I moved down the alley to the next pen after I latched the gate shut. The pen I'd been working was getting full and the calves were trying to go back. Jack still had a lot of room in his pen.

Soon Dennis hollered at Jack, "Here comes your calf! Open up!"

Jack opened his gate and Dennis followed a dwarf calf into the pen.

"Are you sure that's my calf?" asked Jack.

"Certainly!" replied Dennis. "See how small it is!"

"I don't see my brand or my earmark on it," said Jack.

"It has to be your calf," said Dennis. "Look at how small it is!"

"I better take a closer look," said Jack as he closed the gate and entered the pen.

Dennis looked down the alley at me. He had a big smile on his face and winked at me. He was having some fun at Jack's expense.

Jack returned to the gate. "That's your calf, Dennis! It has your brand and earmark on it. You've been fooling me!"

"Just havin' a little fun," said Dennis. "I did see your calf. She's a bigger one. I was really considerin' keepin' her for a replacement!"

"I wouldn't put it past you, you old cow thief!" said Jack.

Dennis smiled and returned to the herd in the big corral. He was pleased that he'd had a little fun at Jack's expense.

We continued sorting calves from cows the rest of the morning. Around noon, Dennis asked, "You wanna take a little break? It's about noon an' we're about half done."

"It wouldn't hurt me," I said. "I feel like I've walked about a million miles!"

"Let's take a break," said Jack. "We need to help out the younger generation."

"If the Missus were here, she'd have somethin' fixed to eat. But I'll see what I can rustle up," said Dennis.

"Rustle up is correct," said Jack. "You're getting pretty good at rustling up. You should get plenty!"

Dennis took his horse to the barn and unsaddled him. "I'll trade horses after we eat," he said.

Jack and I walked to the house while Dennis unsaddled.

When Dennis arrived, he went right to work fixing a noon meal.

While we were eating, Jack said, "This is not a bad meal you've rustled up. Of course, you've had a lot of practice rustling!"

We all laughed and continued eating.

When we were done, Dennis said, "I'm not used to eatin' at noon. I could use a nap! But I'd better not. We need to finish before dark."

Dennis saddled another horse and we returned to the corral and resumed sorting. I had to move down to the next pen as I'd filled up the previous one before we broke for the noon meal. Jack moved down a pen.

Soon, Dennis hollered at Jack, "Here's your calf!"

"I'll look her over real close!" said Jack. "Just hold her in the alley and we'll put her with her mother. The way you're sorting, I don't want them to become separated!"

Both men laughed. The apparent mistake earlier had only eased the work and made the day easier and a little fun. Dennis held the calf in the alley and Jack moved back to the pen that they'd put his cow in.

"That's my calf, all right!" said Jack. He opened the gate. "Put her in here."

Before dark, Dennis said, "I think we've got 'em all sorted. We'll turn out the cows an' put the bulls, cull cows, an' Jack's cow an' calf in the bull pasture. We'll put the calves in the big pen an' feed 'em there. We'll have to hook up the trailer to the tractor an' load up the trailer with hay to feed."

CHAPTER 12

We turned out the cows, Jack and I got our horses and we moved the bulls, cull cows, and Jack's cow and calf to the bull pasture. Dennis counted the cull cows into the pasture. We returned to the corrals, unsaddled and fed our horses, and loaded the trailer with hay.

Dennis drove the tractor and Jack and I forked off hay in the big corral.

"That should hold 'em," said Dennis when we were done.

We turned the calves into the big corral and went to the house. Dennis immediately started fixing supper. He cooked up steaks for everybody.

"These are good steaks," said Jack. "Good enough to be from my cattle. Where did you get them?"

"They came from a steer I butchered last spring. Ranch bred an' raised right here," replied

Dennis. "I don't think I could eat anythin' off your place!"

Both men laughed. The apparent accusations between them about rustling or stealing each other's cattle was taken with a lot of humor. Other men would have taken offense at the remarks, but these two had been friends a long time.

At supper, Dennis said, "Tomorrow we'll sort off the steers from the heifers. When did you say the trucks were comin'?"

"Day after tomorrow," replied Jack. "They should be here around ten in the morning."

"Good," said Dennis. "I counted twenty-three cull cows so we'll have to sort off that many heifers in the mornin'."

Sleep that night didn't come as easy as it should have. All night the calves were bawling for their mothers. After I finally got to sleep, I slept right through the bawling.

The next day we saddled our horses and gathered the bull pasture. As we approached the gate, Jack said, "I'll go ahead and make sure my cow and calf are present."

We put the cattle we'd gathered in a smaller pen and started sorting steers from heifers.

"Pete," said Dennis, "you take the heifers an'

Jack, you take the steers. When I holler 'hold 'em,' you hold the heifer in the alley. I want to look over the heifers pretty close an' pick some good ones for replacements. We'll put the replacements in a separate pen."

We sorted calves all morning only slowing down when Dennis wanted to look over a heifer. If he selected a particular heifer, we penned her separately.

About noon, Dennis asked, "You wanna break for the noon meal? We're about half done an' got plenty of time."

"Sure," said Jack. "Anytime I can get a meal at your expense, I want to take it!"

We went to the house and Dennis fixed up a noon meal. After eating, we continued sorting the calves.

As Dennis put a heifer in the replacement pen, Jack said, "That's twenty-three."

"I'll put one more in the pen," said Dennis. "I can fatten her up an' slaughter her in the spring."

We finished sorting the calves then sorted the bulls from the heifers. Dennis cut seven bulls into the cull pen. We took the remaining bulls back to the bull pasture. We put Jack's cow and calf in a separate pen. When we were done, we turned the horses loose and fed them.

Dennis said, "We need to load the trailer with hay. We'll feed in the north and south big pens, then, after we've put out the hay, we'll turn the heifers in the south pen an' the steers in the north pen. It'll be easier to drive the tractor in the pens without the calves in the way. Then we'll be done for the day."

"Don't forget to feed my cow and your bulls," said Jack.

"Oh!" said Dennis, "I almost forgot!"

We loaded hay onto the trailer and fed in the pens. We also fed Jack's cow and calf with the bulls. We fed the replacements in the pen they were in.

When it was past time for supper, I was tired. During the last two days sorting cattle, I'd done a lot of walking, all in the same area, opening and closing the gate as needed. With all the walking I'd done, I hadn't got anywhere!

At supper, Dennis said, "First thing in the mornin', we'll sort off the bulls an' put what I want to keep back in the bull pasture, if the trucks aren't here yet. We'll spend the rest of the day loadin' cattle. I don't think we'll get 'em all loaded an' shipped in one day."

"The trucking company told me the brand

inspector will be here when the trucks arrive," said Jack.

"I hope he's on time," said Dennis. "We can't load anything until he's looked at 'em."

"Looks like we've got another day workin' on foot," I said. "I'm goin' to hit the sack."

"Breakfast at six," said Dennis.

I nodded sleepily. I'd heard that before.

The next morning while we were eating, we heard trucks pulling into the yard.

"We better hurry and finish breakfast," said Jack.

"There's no rush," said Dennis as he got up and looked out the window. "The brand inspector ain't here. Just finish up."

One of the truck drivers came to the house and Dennis met him at the door.

"You ready to start shipping cattle?" asked the driver.

"Soon as the brand inspector shows up," answered Dennis.

"He's right behind us," said the driver.

"Then get a truck up to the loadin' chute an' we'll get started," said Dennis. "You boys hurry your breakfast. We're ready to start."

We quickly finished eating and went to the

corrals. One of the trucks had backed his trailer up to the loading chute and was ready to start.

On the way to the corrals, we met the brand inspector and the cattle buyer. After introductions all around, Dennis said, "Let's get started. There's a truck at the loadin' chute an' he's ready. We'll start with the steers."

The brand inspector's name was Erving Emerson. He preferred to be called Erv. The cattle buyer's name was Hank Logan.

"The drivers will tell us how many calves he wants for each section of the trailer," said Dennis. Turning to Jack and myself, he said, "You boys count off what the driver tells you an' put 'em in the alley way. The driver will push 'em into the trailer. Erv, you can sit on the fence on the alley way an' look at each calf as they go by. Hank, you an' me can sit by the brand inspector an' make the count. The other drivers can help push the calves onto the trailers. Ready?"

There was a nod of agreement among everyone present.

"Then, let's get started," said Dennis.

We started by putting all the steers into the small pens along each side of the alley. The driver called out how many he wanted for the front compartment and Jack and I counted out that number of calves and put them in the alley. Before the driver had the calves loaded, he called out the number he wanted for the next compartment.

We soon had the first truck loaded and before it even pulled away, the second truck was ready to move into position.

When the truck was loaded, Hank and Dennis compared figures. They matched. There were seventy-two calves on the first truck.

I did some quick figuring and thought we would need ten trucks to haul everything.

Hank and Dennis were doing the same figuring and Hank told the driver of the first truck, "You unload and come straight back here. You'll have to make two trips."

The driver didn't seem to mind and pulled out. The second truck backed into position and we resumed loading the calves.

Jack and I knew how many calves were to go into each section of the trailer and as soon as the driver started loading the first compartment, we started counting out what was needed for the second compartment.

We loaded trailers all day, not stopping for a noon meal until all seven trucks were loaded and gone. When the last truck had left, Erv, Hank,

Jack, Dennis, and I went to the house to get something to eat.

"The way I have it figured, we have about an hour before the first truck is due back," said Hank. "My count shows four hundred and twenty-six steer calves."

"That's what I got," said Dennis. "The rest are heifers. An' we got some of them loaded already. We'll have twenty-three cull cows an' seven bulls to load."

Erv said, "I noticed one of your cows and a calf in a separate pen, Jack. Did you know she was there?"

"Is she?" asked Jack in apparent astonishment. "Do you think Dennis is trying to steal her?" Everyone laughed.

"I wouldn't be surprised," said Erv. "You two guys been stealing each other's cows for years!"

Everyone laughed again. Apparently everyone in the country knew of the joke between Jack and Dennis.

When the trucks started arriving, we went back to loading.

When we had the remaining heifers loaded, it was beginning to get dark. We loaded the cull cows and bulls into the last truck. Erv looked over the corrals that were empty, except for Jack's pair.

"You haven't loaded that cow and calf," said Erv.

"Nope," I said. "But I can get her if you want!"

Everyone laughed. It had been a long, tough day and it was good to end it on a humorous note.

"If you fellers want to stay for supper, I'll fix up somethin' special," said Dennis.

"Nope," said Erv. "My wife will have something special when I get home. By the way, I'm sorry to hear about Peg's passing. I couldn't make the memorial, I had some cattle to inspect on the other side of the county. She was a special woman. You boys take care, I've got to be leaving."

Erv left, but not before Dennis thanked him.

"Those brand inspectors have to look at each critter," said Hank.

"He's a good man an' got a tough job to do," said Dennis.

"I'm surprised he hasn't thrown you and Jack in jail years ago for stealing each other's cattle!" said Hank.

"I guess we're just lucky," said Jack.

Turning to Dennis, Hank said, "I'll have your check ready Monday of next week. Do you want to come and get it or do you want me to mail it to you?"

"I better come an' get it," said Dennis. "But I've got to help Jack ship his calves before I come to town."

"And he has to return my cow and calf!" said Jack.

"When you get to town, your check will be ready at my office," said Hank.

Hank turned to Jack and said, "When will you have your calves ready to ship?"

"Give me a day to gather, a day to sort and we'll be ready the next day," said Jack. "If my help shows up on time!"

"We'll be there on time, won't we Pete!" retorted Dennis.

"I'll bet we'll be early," I said.

"Okay," said Hank. "Three days from now, the trucks will be at your place. Are the roads still as rough?"

"Yes," replied Jack. "You know I don't have a car. No need to improve the roads."

"Well then," said Hank, "The trucks will be there after noon. We'll see you then."

Hank left and the three of us started to the house. "If you want your cow fed, better feed her," said Dennis. "Pete an' me will feed the horses."

Jack left to feed his cow and calf. Dennis and I fed the horses and met Jack at the house. Dennis immediately started supper.

While eating, Dennis said, "Tomorrow we'll load my black horse an' Pete, you load Bay Boy an' we'll go to Jack's an' give him a hand with his shippin'. You want to ride in the truck over to your place, Jack?"

"No," said Jack. "I'll ride my horse."

Dennis asked, "How come?"

"The ride is smoother and easier on my horse," replied Jack. "I'll leave when you leave and get there before you do. I also want to make sure my cow and calf gets loaded. I can see to that before I leave."

"Still don't trust me, huh?" questioned Dennis.

"Certainly not!" replied Jack, grinning.

"We'll turn my horses loose in the bull pasture. I'll keep in the two we use at Jack's over the winter, just in case I need 'em. We'll be at your place when we get there. Make sure you load your bedroll, Pete. We'll be there three days, maybe longer. We'll put our bedrolls on the headache rack over the cab of the truck."

The next morning, while we were saddling horses, Jack said, "If you load my cow and calf and your horses, you can drive to the bull pasture and I can follow your horses to the bull pasture. If you open the gate, I'll put them in there."

"I bet we can do that," said Dennis.

We did as planned and Jack left on his horse to go to his place and Dennis and I drove to Jack's. From the previous trip to Jack's, I knew it would take us some time to get there and I knew Jack would beat us home.

While driving to Jack's, Dennis said, "I did some figurin' last night an' figure I got about a ninety-five percent calvin' percentage. That ain't too bad for calvin' out in the open."

"It's really hard to get a hundred percent," I said.

When we arrived at Jack's, he was fixing a noon meal. We ate after unloading our horses and the cow and calf.

"We can gather and start sorting now if you want," said Jack.

"Might just as well," said Dennis. "Our horses are already saddled. You don't have as many cattle as I do so it shouldn't take us long."

"Of course, we'll have to load hay and feed them when we're done," said Jack.

"There's always a negative side to helpin' you out," said Dennis.

We gathered Jack's cattle off the hay fields

we'd put them on some days previously. It wasn't a tough gather, Jack only had about half as many cows as Dennis. As soon as the cattle were corralled in a larger pen, we started sorting. It was much the same as it had been at Dennis's except that Jack did the sorting. Dennis and I operated the gates as Jack called out "cow" or "calf."

At one point, Jack hollered, "That's your cow and calf, Dennis! Pen her separately!"

"That's a good cow," said Dennis as the cow entered an empty pen. "An' the calf is even better! It's just like you to steal one of my best cows, Jack!"

Both men laughed, and penned the pair separately.

By dark, we had all the calves separated. We turned the cows back out on the hay field, loaded hay onto a trailer and scattered it out in the large pen. Then we put the calves in the larger pen, unsaddled our horses, turned them loose in a pen and threw them some hay.

I hadn't noticed, but there was a new truck in front of Jack's house.

"I have a surprise for you," said Jack.

"What is it?" asked Dennis.

"My sister and her husband have come out to cook for us," replied Jack.

"You mean Maria's here?" questioned Dennis. "It'll be nice to see her again. It's been some time since I've seen her. That's a nice surprise. Her cookin' is a lot better than yours an' yours ain't as good as mine!"

"Yes," answered Jack. "And she'll be here for the next three days. Her husband can help us tomorrow."

Maria met us at the door. There was a nice reunion between Maria and Dennis. It was apparent they'd been good friends in the past. I was introduced to her husband, Ben Nighthorse.

"Jack told me you were goin' to cook for us the next three days," Dennis said to Maria.

"Yes," replied Maria. "I knew that you were coming and that Peggy wouldn't be here, so I took a few days off from the bank to come out here and take care of you boys. And Jack needed some groceries to get through the winter."

"That's mighty nice," said Dennis. "Nicer than Jack would have treated us!"

CHAPTER 13

After a fantastic meal that Maria fixed, we discussed the activities planned for the next day. The procedure would be pretty much the same as when we worked Dennis's cattle.

At one point, Jack said, "Get your bedroll, Pete. I'll show you where you can stay. Bring it in the house."

I did as I was told and Jack led me to a room at the end of a hall.

"This is where you can stay," he said as he opened the door. "Ben and Maria will be down the hall and Dennis will be in the next room. There's a private bathroom through that door. The thermostat for heat is on that wall."

It was a little cool in the room and Jack turned the heat up.

"You can adjust that to where you want it when it warms up," he said.

"This is a lot better than I expected," I said.

"I have all the comforts of the white man, electric heat and lights, indoor plumbing, a telephone, everything," said Jack. "There's a television over there and you can set it to turn off automatically when you want. Just make yourself at home."

"I might get too comfortable," I said.

"That's all right," replied Jack. "You get settled in and you can come and visit with us if you wish, or turn in. We'll have breakfast at seven."

"That's an hour later than at Dennis's, I said. "I'll be up earlier than that."

"If you're up earlier, just come to the kitchen. Coffee will be ready. I expect everyone will be up before six."

"I think I'll turn in now," I said. "The ride up that road was a little tough."

"Fine," said Jack. "See you in the morning. We've got the calves sorted off the cows. Tomorrow, we'll separate the steers from the heifers. You won't need your horse. The next day, we'll bring in the cows and cut off some cull cows. You'll need your horse then."

"What about replacement heifers?" I asked.

"I won't need any," answered Jack. "I held over more heifers than I needed last year and actually have more cows than I can handle. We'll see you in the morning."

I turned in after watching the news. I was content. I had a room by myself and a private bathroom. I'd never had that kind of luxury before.

The next day we separated steers from heifers. Dennis and I worked the gates. Jack brought out the calves, one at a time, and Ben, mounted on one of Jack's horses, brought them down the alley.

Around noon, Maria came to the corrals. "Your dinner is ready now," she said. Her tone of voice was more like an order to come and eat, rather than an invitation.

"I guess we better go eat now," said Jack.

Jack and Ben turned their horses loose in an empty pen and we all followed Maria to the house.

After a big noon meal, Jack said, "I'm full! We need to take it easy for an hour or so, just to let things settle."

We all sat down in the living room. I was busy looking around, taking in all the Indian decoration. Ben fell asleep. Dennis, Maria, and Jack visited.

When we all went back to sorting the calves, it didn't take long to finish. When we were done, we loaded a trailer with hay, fed the calves and went to the house. We still had an hour or so before supper and I went to my room and layed down to rest. I fell asleep.

I was awakened by a knock on the door and Jack saying, "It's time for supper!"

I woke up, feeling foolish that I'd fallen asleep. I went to supper still a little drowsy.

The next day, we saddled our horses and brought the cows in.

I worked the gate for the cull cows. Jack and Dennis cut out the culls and Ben brought them down the alley to my pen. When we had about twenty cows we stopped.

"That's all," said Jack.

We turned the cows back onto the hay field and rode to the ranch.

Maria had the noon meal ready. As we were eating Jack said, "We don't have anything to do the rest of the day, other than load up some hay and feed the calves. We'll do that, then load up some to feed in the morning. Then all we can do is wait for the trucks."

"Aren't you goin' to feed my cow an' calf?" asked Dennis.

"You can do that," replied Jack.

While we were eating the noon meal the next

day, the trucks started showing up, along with Hank and Erv.

Loading the calves, we followed the same procedure as we did when loading Dennis's calves. By dark, we had all the calves and cull cows loaded.

Erv turned to Jack and said, "I see you have one of Dennis's pairs in a pen. Do you plan on returning the pair to its rightful owner?"

"Of course," answered Jack. "That pair was my insurance that I'd get my pair back!"

Everyone laughed at the humor of the situation, knowing that neither man would steal the other man's cattle.

Erv left and before Hank left, he asked Jack, "Do you want me to mail your check or do you want to come to town and get it?"

"You know I don't come to town. When you go to the bank, just give it to Maria. She can deposit it into my account."

"Dennis," said Hank, "your check is at my office. When do you want to get it?"

"We'll be in town day after tomorrow," answered Dennis. "I'll pick it up then."

"Your calves weighed up pretty well, Dennis," said Hank. "Your check is pretty sizeable!"

"Good!" replied Dennis. "I need the money!"

Hank left.

Jack turned to Dennis and said, "You might just as well spend the night here. It'll be pretty late by the time you got to your place if you left now."

"Yep," said Dennis. "Another meal of Maria's wouldn't hurt me none!"

Maria had a big supper ready when we got to the house. After supper, I turned in. The morning had been pretty easy with not much to do, but the afternoon had been hectic and I was tired.

The next morning, Dennis and I saddled our horses. We put our bedrolls on the headache rack, loaded the horses and Dennis's cow and calf.

Before we left, Dennis asked Jack, "Can you call the vet? I'll want to pregnancy check the cows about the first of December. Let me know when he can come."

"Sure," replied Jack. "I'll let you know."

We climbed into the truck and started toward Dennis's ranch. On the way, I said, "That Ben don't say much."

"No," answered Dennis. "But he's a good hand. He helps Jack out quite a bit, irrigatin', fixin' fence, odd jobs. Maria's really the brains in the family. She's got a job at the bank, head teller, I think. She has hopes of becomin' the bank president someday. But I don't think she'll make it."

"Really! How come?" I interrupted.

"Too much prejudice against Indians," answered Dennis.

"That's why Jack told Hank to give his check to Maria," I said.

"Yep! She'll make sure it gets deposited in the right account. She keeps an eye on Jack's money for him. I think he's got a pretty sizeable amount of money stored there."

We got to Dennis' ranch, turned the cow and calf out, unsaddled the horses and fed them. Our chores were done for the day.

At supper, Dennis asked me, "Now that we're done, what are your plans? I'd kinda like for you to stick around, help with the preg checkin' an' help me feed this winter. You've got a job if you want it."

"I appreciate it," I said. "But I kinda thought I'd like to spend the winter where it's warmer. It's been plenty cold already here."

"You think about it. You've got a job if you want it an' some good horses to ride an' not really much work to do."

"I'll think on it," I said.

The next morning, after feeding the horses, Dennis said, "You might just as well ride into town with me. There ain't nothin' to do out here."

We got into the car and drove to town. All the way to town, Dennis tried to convince me to stay on for the winter. He even got to the point where he offered to sell me the place, "at a good price" when he was ready to retire.

To his offer, I replied, "I ain't ready for that, yet." Trying to change the subject, I said, "You didn't follow the trucks to watch the calves being weighed. How come?"

"Hank's been buying my calves for years. He's as honest as the day's long. I consigned my calves to him last spring at a pretty good price an' he's always treated me right." Dennis appeared satisfied with the arrangement.

Our first stop in town was at Hank's office. Hank wasn't there, but his secretary cheerfully handed over an envelope with Dennis's name on it.

Dennis opened up the envelope and looked at the figures. "The calves did weigh up nicely," he said. "Better than last year."

"I have last year's figures available if you want to see them and compare," said Hank's secretary.

"Thank you," said Dennis, "that's not necessary."

We left the office and our next stop was at the bank.

Dennis was greeted with a "Hello Mister Jorgenson," from everyone at the bank. He was well known.

"I'd like to see Maria Nighthorse," Dennis told one of the tellers.

"She's in a meeting," the teller responded. "She'll be available shortly. Can anyone else help you?"

"No," answered Dennis. "We'll just wait."

We sat down in some overstuffed chairs. They were comfortable and I thought that I could easily fall asleep in one of them if I was tired.

Maria emerged from her conference shortly and approached us.

"Mister Jorgenson, it's so nice to see you again," she said, extending her hand. "How may I help you?"

"I have some business to transact with you this morning," said Dennis, shaking Maria's hand.

"Come over to my desk and have a seat," said Maria.

Maria was formal with Dennis, calling him Mister Jorgenson. At Jack's ranch, it had been on a first name basis. At Maria's desk, it became informal.

"I suppose you want to deposit Hank's check, Dennis."

"Yeah, Maria," said Dennis. "An' I need to pay Pete here, but I forgot my checkbook."

I heard that and immediately thought I'd have to spend more time at the ranch waiting for my money. I was ready to leave.

"We can get a counter check for you to pay Pete," said Maria. "That won't be a problem."

I was relieved when I heard that.

"Endorse Hank's check. I'll look up your account, give you a deposit slip and a counter check," said Maria, reaching into her desk for the items.

Dennis signed his check and Maria handed him a counter check, saying, "Be sure to deduct Pete's social security before you make out the check."

I was a little disappointed to hear that.

Dennis asked, "How do you figure that? Peg always handled that sort of stuff."

Maria reached into a lower drawer of her desk. "I have a table in this book, it'll show you how much to take out. You'll have to send that amount to the Social Security Administration."

"Can you do that for me, Maria?" asked Dennis.

"Sure. How much do you owe Pete?"

Dennis told her what my total wages were. Maria entered that figure into the calculator on her desk then ran her finger down the chart. She stopped and subtracted that figure from the number on the calculator. She entered two figures on a piece of paper and handed it to Dennis.

All this figuring was done in silence and I had the thought occur to me that I might owe Dennis!

Giving the paper to Dennis, she said, "This is what you owe Pete and this is what you owe the Social Security Administration. You'll need two counter checks."

Pete made out a counter check to me and handed it over.

"You can cash it at one of the teller stations, Pete," said Maria.

I took the check and looked at it. It wasn't as much as I figured, the Social Security that was taken out made up the difference. But the check was big enough that I thought I could live on it until I found another job in a warmer climate.

I cashed the check and put the money in my shirt pocket. I'd left my wallet in the car back at the ranch. I returned to Maria's desk where Dennis was taking care of his business.

Maria was saying, "You need to be sure to enter your deposit in your checkbook and subtract Pete's check and your payment to Social Security."

"I'll forget that by the time I get to the ranch," said Dennis.

"I'll give you a new bank book and put your balance in it," said Maria.

After visiting with Maria and thanking her for cooking at Jack's, we concluded our business at the bank and left.

"Anythin' you need in town?" asked Dennis.

My reply was simple. "Nope."

"Apparently, I haven't convinced you to stay on for the winter," said Dennis.

"Nope," I replied.

"Well, I better go to the employment office an' look for some winter help," said Dennis.

"Yeah," I said. I thought I might look for another job farther south while we were there.

At the employment office, I looked over the jobs posted on a bulletin board, while Dennis talked with an employment counselor. There were some jobs available south of here, but not far enough south. I wanted to go to Arizona, New Mexico, or Southern California.

On the ride back to the ranch, Dennis tried to convince me to stay for the winter, but I was firm on leaving. When we got to the ranch, it was late afternoon.

Dennis said, "You might just as well spend the night here an' leave in the mornin' after breakfast."

"Thanks," I said. "I appreciate that."

After supper, I started gathering up my stuff and loading it in the car. My stuff consisted of mostly dirty laundry. I would take my shaving gear and bedroll to the car in the morning.

At breakfast, Dennis had pretty well given up on convincing me to stay.

He followed me to the bunkhouse. I loaded my shaving gear and bedroll in the car. I was going to drive to the barn to get my saddle, but Dennis was right on my heels, so I walked.

At the barn, I slung my chaps over my shoulder, put my blankets and pad under one arm, got my saddle with my free hand and started toward the car.

Dennis asked, "Can I take some of that for you?"

"Nope," I replied. I was going to ask, "Take it permanently?" but decided against it. I wanted to leave on good terms.

I put my saddle and equipment in the trunk of the car and turned to Dennis.

"It's time, old timer," I said, sticking out my hand.

"You sure you want to go?" said Dennis grabbing my hand. As firm as his grip was, I thought he wasn't going to let me go.

"I'm sure," I replied. "I hope I did you a good job!"

Letting my hand go, he said, "You did! You know, you've always got a job here anytime you want it!"

"Thanks," I said as I got into the car. "I'll remember that!"

Dennis stepped away from the car and I started it. As I drove off I saw him in the mirror waving his hand. I stuck my arm out the window and waved back. I watched him in the mirror and thought he looked like a forlorn, lonely old man. I felt sorry for him thinking he might have to spend the winter alone. I almost turned back, but didn't. I was on my way to a warmer climate!

THE END

Other Books by Stu Campbell

Horsing Around a Lot
Horsing Around the Dudes
Humor Around Horses
You Can't Be Serious!
Comedy Around the Corral
More Humor Around Horses
Muddy Waters
Comedy Around Cowboys
The Loner
The Drifter
The Life of a Cowboy
The Wagon

A Young Cowboy's Adventure Series

A Young Cowboy's Adventure
Honey
Surprise!
Intruders
Expectations
Frozen
Advice
Broken
Ginny

Wild Horses for Wild Kids
The Kids Get Horses

About the Author

Stu bases his books on his true-life experiences of ranch life and being a cowboy. He is a graduate of Utah State University with a degree in Animal Husbandry, and has also been a ski instructor, truck driver, and rancher.

About the Cover Artist

Cowboy artist, **R. Loren Schmidt**, is truly a cowboy and an artist. He illustrates from real life experiences from his lifetime of cowboying. A lifetime of dedicated art practice is evident in his expressive and accurate depictions of the contemporary cowboy experience. Loren is most inspired by his friends, horses, and the grand adventures in the backcountry of the West.